The Machine

j. manoa

EPIC
Press

The Machine
The One: Book #3

Written by J. Manoa

Copyright © 2016 by Abdo Consulting Group, Inc.

Published by EPIC Press™
PO Box 398166
Minneapolis, MN 55439

Printed in the United States of America.

Cover design by Candice Keimig
Images for cover art obtained from iStockPhoto.com
Edited by Ryan Hume

Library of Congress Cataloging-in-Publication Data

Manoa, J.
The machine / J. Manoa.
p. cm. — (The one; #3)
Summary: Far from the family who had secretly monitored him, armed guards follow Odin's every movement through an underground facility dedicated to the secret project known only as Solar Flare. Odin is subjected to daily experiments, which push his powers to their very limits and beyond. Meanwhile, Wendell continues to influence doubt and suspicion directly into Odin's mind forcing him to question who to trust or how to escape.
ISBN 978-1-68076-052-1 (hardcover)
1. Imaginary playmates—Fiction. 2. Interpersonal relations—Fiction.
3. Family life—Fiction. 4. Friendship—Fiction. 5. Psychic ability—Fiction.
6. Young adult fiction. I. Title.
[Fic]—dc23
2015949419

To my big brother, I'll always look up to you

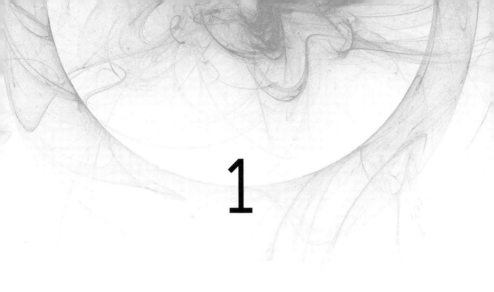

1

"**I** TRUST YOU'RE ENJOYING THIS NEW ARRANGEMENT, Odin?"

Lieutenant General Edward Delgado leans back to survey the room. His chair and mine are bolted onto two rails placed under the floor. The other two chairs, one on each side, have yet to be used since I moved into this living area nine days ago. The table between us is soldered into place.

"Time was, I had to share such a place with five hundred other cadets."

He looks almost wistfully at the entertainment center at the front of the room. A larger television than I've ever seen before is embedded into the wall. The soldered coffee table and bolted couch which face the TV are visible upon entrance through the two-inch thick door with the touch screen identification system that only eight people are fingerprint-coded to enter. There is no access to live broadcasts, but the internal hard drive is stocked with hundreds of movies, television shows, albums, and other media. The whole system is operated by voice: "TV on," "TV volume up," "TV movies browse," "TV shows search," "TV off," etc.

"Even then it wasn't quite so . . . convenient," Delgado says, moving his view from the front of the room to the back, the fitness area. Four exercise machines, two stationary bikes and two treadmills, also soldered to the floor. I've used one of the bikes a few times but usually I'm too fatigued or annoyed after testing to do anything but rest.

"Yet, here you are with this entire place all to yourself . . . " he says. He tilts his head to see the shelf embedded into the wall passed me. The books and board games are stored behind the same glass as the cameras in each corner. I have to get one of my guards to open it anytime I want to read or Dr. Burnett wants to reminisce. A guard remains in the room with me until any removed item is returned. They don't want anything loose. Nothing that I might be able to use against them.

" . . . While young men and women not much older than yourself are jammed together in much less lavish quarters without complaint." He concludes, "You should consider yourself fortunate."

"One major difference between me and the rest of them," I reply, glancing over Delgado's shoulder to the eight fully-armed, fully-armored soldiers a few steps behind him, head to foot in desert camouflage, including the light brown masks which hide their faces, "is that they volunteered."

"Exactly my point," he says, the melodic tones of his voice betraying the rigid lines and sharp angles of his face. "Those men and women choose to serve. They don't need to be coddled into serving their country." He opens his arms to indicate the soldiers lining up behind him. "They don't see any shame in their service."

"Then why wear the masks?"

One ridge-like vein pulses slightly through the jagged canyons of his forehead. "Those are to keep you from doing your mindreading, or whatever it is, on them. In fact," he looks around the room once again, "everything in here is made specifically to cater to you. This entire facility, billions of tax-payer dollars in construction and technology and other luxuries, have been dedicated to making you feel the same sense of pride and duty as thousands of your contemporaries feel for nothing more than the opportunity to serve." He frowns, even more noticeably than usual. "Is that fair to you?"

"I've also had my entire life planned to condition me into accepting my place here, General. Does that seem fair to you? In fact, unlike the brave men of your entourage, I can't remember a time in my entire life when I was able to actually choose anything."

He inhales as if about to speak.

"Oh wait," I say, "it was this morning. I chose the omelet for breakfast. It was . . . " His eyes are razors scraping along the edges of my face. " . . . Damp."

He shows a one-sided smile, lines around his eyes like crags carved into his skin. "I've known kids like you before. Clever ones. You know what clever gets you in the real world?"

"Ummm . . . " I make a show of thinking about it. "Is it killed? I bet it's killed."

"Nothing," he says. "Absolutely nothing. I have no tolerance for things that do nothing. Now this," he gestures out to the room around us, "this is something. Something that has cost a lot of time and a lot of money to construct. *This*," he gestures outwardly again, "is a promise. It is a promise to every man, woman, and child in this country that we will do everything we can to protect them." His eyes narrow to slivers dug into rock. "And I have even less tolerance for anyone who would stand in the way of fulfilling that promise."

He cuts me off this time.

"Now the good doctor and her fellow *researchers*," he pronounces the word as though it was profane, drawing a division between those who study and those who act, "believe that these abilities of yours may be able to save the world through some pie-in-the-sky idealism, but me, all I care about are results. We've seen some impressive things these last two weeks, that's true, and that's why you have been allowed free reign over this palace." He leans toward me, arms on the table, like a railroad spike being driven forward. "But do not delude yourself for one second that I will not send you right back into that hellhole of a cell if you show even the inclination of skirting the responsibility you have to the men, women, and children of this country. I have no need for useless things. I would rather this venture fail than see more time and resources poured into some fanciful wish for a better tomorrow."

I clench my teeth and stare back at him, despite

knowing that even if he were to punch me, the guns behind him would assure that I do nothing but take the hit.

"And how you show that to me," he says, sitting back again, "is in that laboratory every day. Show me you deserve to be here." He indicates the room again. The common room, as Burnett ironically calls it. "Or you will not be here much longer. That is my promise to you."

The basketball floats about five feet in the air and just out of arm's reach. I keep my hand out, picturing the motion needed to arc the ball toward the hoop fifteen feet away. The last time I was tested at shooting free throws was in eighth grade when the gym coach was trying to recruit for the boys' team. I went two for ten and didn't make it, which was fine because I was too short anyway. I adjust the placement of the ball, and when it looks about right, use the air to slowly guide the ball toward the hoop, adjusting at it goes. It's a lot like my birthday bowling "party" except that the ball is under my control the whole time. The shot moves in slow motion to the hoop and I let it drop in. Fifty-three straight. I could go pro with this kind of skill. If I weren't stuck here.

"How does that feel, Odin?" says Dr. Winger from behind the bulletproof glass looking into the testing lab. "Difficult?"

"No." I say loudly back. I still don't know exactly where the microphones are in the room. Unlike the equipment carted in through the observer-side door, I haven't seen the sound receivers.

I don't need to see Delgado to know he's standing against the wall several feet back and to the right of Dr. Winger. Delgado's always there during testing, staring at me wherever I go, a statue from his stance to his stone face.

Winger sits behind the console. He glances between me in the room and the monitoring equipment. The cameras catch my external actions, the way I move to help my mind simulate the desired action and the expressions I make when manipulating objects into place. The black lines gridded through the white room track the speed of every object. Pressure gauges wired through each surface register any force my efforts generate. There are, of course, the sound receivers for any noise. Most importantly for them, the five electrodes attached to my head create multiple images of my brain function, which Winger and his two assistants record and transmit to someone else, someone whom I've never seen and therefore can't read.

After three weeks of typically two testing sessions per day, I've become so accustomed to having these wires on my head that I barely notice them anymore. What I do notice, every day, is the shaved look, which I hadn't done since I moved into Ben and Aida's house. The soldier who first shaved my head commented, "Now you look like a recruit."

"I suppose I do," I replied, conscious of the contrast between my orange jumpsuit and his brown shirt and desert camo pants.

"You have a really round head," he continued. "A lot of these guys come here, get their first cut, and learn they have weird bumps in their skulls. But yours is perfectly round."

"Thanks, I guess," I said.

This was the day after Burnett explained the testing arrangement which sprung me from the tiny cell in the detention area of the complex. She phrased it as a choice, "If you do this, then you will receive that," as though we were equals. I still march past detention every time I go to and from the lab or the mess, as if the floor plan of this facility were made to remind me of where I'll go if I don't cooperate with Delgado's tests.

I pick up the next ball from the dozen scattered around the testing lab and place it for another shot. I hear a slight click as Dr. Winger presses the open channel button on the console. Next comes his voice, slow and clear like an old radio announcer through the speakers in each corner and the center of the room. "Try throwing this one," he says. "Release it like a shot and don't guide it."

I nod.

I line the ball up as best I can and try to judge the amount of force needed to reach the basket. It's odd not being able to use muscle memory to determine how hard to throw it. I imagine the ball taking off like a standard pass. The ball sails through the air perfectly straight and perfectly still, no spin and no drift. And then falls about two feet short of the rim. There goes my streak. The ball bounces off the ground and rolls under the basket until it hits the balls that successfully dropped into the hoop.

"Again please," says Winger. "We're not testing accuracy."

Today is the first time they've used basketballs. They started me with very basic things: floating and turning different metal shapes one by one. Move a little block over here. Turn it in the air. Lift this bar and rotate it. Basics. In the same way that every new school year spends the first month rehashing the previous year for the kids who spent the entire summer forgetting everything they'd learned.

Easy as the tasks could be, five to seven hours of intense concentration becomes tiring. By the end of some days I feel like I've taken the SAT twice with no prep or indication of whether the answers are correct or not. At least, until the day the soldiers finally marched me out from the detention cell and across the waiting room to the apartment behind the large door I'd seen so often. Walking into the common room for the first time, I was like a starving man being offered a buffet. I wanted to enjoy everything as quickly as possible. Only after did I realize the catch.

I line up the basketball again and again. I adjust the force from the previous shots. Finally, after five attempts, the ball bounces off the back of the rim and into the net. I throw a fist up in triumph. Behind the glass I can see Winger pump his fist slightly. Delgado does nothing. Winger spins his finger over his head to signal that I should keep going. The next three shots are duplicates: swish. Nothing but net.

Winger presses the button to speak. "Very good," he says. "Now let's forget about the hoop and just launch the ball as hard as you can at the wall."

"As hard as I can?"

"Everything you got," he says, a toothy smile showing through his thick, reddish beard. "Let it rip."

While pursuing his undergraduate degree, Wilfred Winger worked part-time for a shoe store. He was fired after less than three months because a series of female customers complained that he touched their feet in ways which made them uncomfortable.

I pick up one of the balls from under the basket and bring it up my eye level a couple feet ahead. "Which way?" I ask, looking at the glass. Winger points in the direction away from the hoop, the opposite wall about fifty feet in the distance. I keep the ball in the air as I turn. Hawthorne and Perry, Winger's two assistants, hold their tablets to their chests as they scramble from that side of the room in the way they would trying to avoid being caught in a picture, or a firing range.

I nod. I stand as though throwing a chest pass. The one thing I was good at in basketball was passing, especially when my teammates didn't expect it. I could picture exactly where they were going to be and could get the ball there right when needed.

I imagine the ball flying from in front of me. I take a breath and shove both of my hands out so hard I feel my right bicep overextend. The ball launches toward the wall like a bullet. Then it slows after about forty feet. It bounces to the wall with a soft hop.

In the observation room, Winger glances back to Delgado. Delgado does nothing. Winger places one finger in the air. I nod. He shakes his fist. He wants force this time.

I position another ball. I close my eyes and take

a deep breath. "No matter," I whisper to myself. "No matter." It's harder to picture motion, but I try. I want the ball to hit with such force it dents the wall and never touches the ground again. I take another breath.

I take two quick steps. I scream. I shove my arms forward. All I see is an orange streak and an explosion. The ball bounces off the wall and ricochets backward. It drops to the ground like a chunk of tire tossed onto the freeway.

Hawthorne is slack-jawed. Perry has backed into the corner on the far side of the room. Winger stands behind the console, upright and blinking in disbelief. Delgado is unmoved. Winger presses the channel button. "Replay that please." He begins to sit. "Not you, Odin. Hawthorne, replay the feed."

The three scientists stare at their various screens as my previous throw runs again. They're similar in stunned expressions.

"Good?" I say.

Winger presses the button. "Oh, yeah," he says,

"and a good finish for the day. Just be careful removing the sensors and we'll see you tomorrow."

I don't bother asking what these tests are for and they don't bother telling me. We all understand that I'll know whatever I want whenever I want.

"All right," I say, already squeezing the little suction cups attached to my head.

"Thanks, Odin."

Delgado says one word to Winger and leaves through the door masked to look like the rest of the wall in back of the observation room. I don't know why they tried to disguise the door when I can see them open it.

His word was, "Continue."

―――――――⌣―――――――

The early shift is Sergeants McPherson and Rogers. They don't wear the masks that Delgado's personal cadre does. In fact, no one else in the facility is masked. The techs, the cooks, the few other guards, or the late shift of Carter and Harris, no masks for any of them. Only Delgado's guys. Guess he doesn't care if I can do my "mindreading or whatever it is" to them.

Rogers is a recent addition to the guard rotation. He originally joined the service during the wave of patriotism that swelled following September 11th. He got into some heated debates with his fellow soldiers when their unit was shifted from the mission in Kabul to Kirkuk. Many weren't happy to withdraw before their mission was done. Rogers contended that they should stop complaining and follow orders. That attitude suits him well for this assignment. He was sent home after taking two bullets in his right leg. He still walks with a slight limp. McPherson is a twenty-year vet for whom this highly classified assignment is considered a service reward. In Iraq, he shot a man in the head who he believed was approaching his unit with an improvised explosive device stashed in his coat. It was a baby girl he'd found in the street. The man was bringing her to the soldiers so she wouldn't be accidentally killed.

The soldiers flank me immediately after I step out of the testing room door.

"What was it today?" McPherson asks, his gun angled up to the ceiling.

"Shooting free throws."

"Like basketball?"

"Yeah, like basketball."

We walk straight across the small room back to the elevator. The two of them remain one pace behind me on either side. Rogers keeps both hands on his rifle as we walk. He doesn't ask questions.

"But with your brain?"

"Pretty much."

"Man," McPherson shakes his head, "must be something to see."

"It is," I say. And if I tried to show him, he'd shoot me.

On the wall to our right we pass the entrance to the fabrication area, with its camera and screen checkpoint lock like the one in front of my quarters. Other than Delgado, no military personnel are allowed beyond that point. At least none that are currently stationed here. We wait for the elevator at the end of the blank, white room. There are other elevators in the complex, leading to emergency exits back to the surface of the base, but I have yet to actually see them.

"So, what's it feel like to do that?" McPherson asks as we enter the elevator. The two of them enter after me and walk past before turning to the front. He's asked me this same question twice before. It's become our Tuesday morning ritual. Rogers presses the button for level three: living quarters. Level four is testing, level one is entrance; I don't know levels two or five.

"Nothing really. Just think of something and do it."

"Anything?"

"Not exactly."

"Man," he says, "must really be something."

The elevator door opens. It's funny to think this hall was once obscured by a tight march of a dozen guards. It's still as pristine and white as it was that first day, almost unreal in how blank it is. Yet where it was once overwhelmingly new, it's now boring with sameness. We pass through the first of the cross sections, where the halls split into the medical facilities on the left and the communal bathrooms and several small, shared bedrooms on the right, for those staff who are required to stay overnight. We travel straight on to the next cross section, where the waiting area opens up and splits into three directions. A few noisy technicians take an early lunch in the mess hall on the left. Straight ahead are the double security doors leading to the detention area. To the right is the pathway to my living quarters. McPherson presses his palm into the scanner in front of the steel door, which has teeth that open like the jaws of some tremendous beast lying on its side. There's the couch and coffee table in front of the television. We turn down the short path to my personal living space.

McPherson nods as we reach the entrance. I nod back and reach out to the only door I am able to open in the entire facility. Everything else is scanners, keypads, and cameras, but my room, just turn and enter. It's strangely comforting to do so. McPherson and Rogers remain outside.

"See ya later," I say as I shut the door.

"We'll be here," McPherson says just before it closes. They will be, until two in the afternoon, when Sergeants Carter and Harris begin their shift.

"Home again," I mutter as I flip the light on.

Not for long.

"Better than it was," I say freely, without cameras or microphones to pick up our conversation. That's part of Project Solar Flare's effort to make me feel less like a prisoner and more like a participant. One of these luxuries Delgado has so generously granted me because I "choose" to cooperate.

Do not grow too content here.

"I don't think that will be much of a problem." I remove my slippers and leave them next to the door. I wonder how extensive the testing will have to get before they offer me covered footwear. *They.*

The walls of the room are just as empty as any other, but the faux wood grain pattern makes it feel cooler and more comfortable than the stark white walls of the holding cell. The larger bed with a pillow that isn't a slab of foam and sheets that aren't repurposed newspaper help a lot, too. There's even a table with a chair. The table is soldered to the floor, the chair is on encased rails, and I'm not allowed to bring any books or writing utensils in here from the common room, but I guess if I ever feel like doing something other than sleeping, showering, and having at least four eyes following my every motion, I could it in this chair at this table. Still better than the holding cell. Delgado's right about that.

You know what they're doing.

"Yes." I step into the bathroom to wash my hands and face. "I figured it out long before you told me." The shower is how Ben described those in Korea: a shower head on the wall with no curtail or tub to contain the water. It sprays on the floor and down the drain. "Nothing that can be easily broken," I say. Thankfully the floor is dry from the daily cleaning/search of the room while I'm gone. Room service/inspection is one of those benefits/conditions of my participation/capture. I wash my hands in the sink and splash some water on my face. "No possible projectiles." I check out the scar under my eye in the polished metal sheet that constitutes a mirror. The scar has healed into a neat sliver that follows the curve of the orbital bone beneath it. "They want me to feel like I'm privileged to be treated this way and afraid to lose everything I've worked for." It still kinda freaks me out when I see myself with a shaved head, as perfectly round as it may be. I toss some water on my dome. Mostly because I can. "This way I'll be more obliged to follow orders." At least drying is easy. Ten seconds of scrubbing or shaking and done. Perfectly dry. "Basic carrot and stick psychology," I say, stepping out of the bathroom.

More docile. Animals are always easier to contain when they do not see the bars.

"There are still plenty of bars."

Never forget that.

It actually feels weird not having the cameras and speaker in the ceiling. Then it feels weirder to think that it feels weird not to be watched or spoken to by anonymous people any time of the day or night. Funny how quickly we adjust to extreme circumstances, and how slowly we adjust back to more regular ones.

Regardless what they try to convince you of, never forget what they are doing.

"I know exactly what's happening. And in the meantime, I'm learning."

I get that old surge of a single Wendell chuckle starting in the center of my mind and rippling through my whole body.

Good. Continue.

2

"**D**ON'T MOVE THE PIECE THAT WAY." DR. BURNETT motions for me to return the marble to its spot. "Move it the other way."

I gesture one finger to move the marble back to its starting position in my corner and again to hop it over another into the neutral area.

"That's so cool," Dr. Burnett says, her eyebrows raised. "I know it's probably common for you by now, but, c'mon, you have to admit that it's very cool."

"I guess so," I say flatly.

"You guess so? Odin, you are able to do things with your mind that no one else we yet know of can." She mimics my tone, "I guess so." She keeps her hands folded in front of her. Her eyes are soft and understanding. Not sure if the look is natural or trained.

We sit at the same table in the common room where Delgado and I were almost exactly twenty-four hours ago. Burnett has to get one of my guards to let her into the living quarters during our scheduled sessions. The guards then remain outside the door until she presses the button to request exit. This is designed to make me feel comfortable. She moves her furthest piece out to set up a long jump chain toward the other side.

"No one else yet?" I say. I rub my arm where it still hurts from yesterday's test.

"Seven billion people and growing," she says. "Stands to logic that at least one other person within that vast number would be as interesting as you."

I'm five years old again, playing Chinese checkers in her office. Even though the opposing sides are green and red, she still chooses to play yellow. "I'm a rebel," she joked while loading the pieces onto her side. "Just don't tell my superiors." I move my front marble diagonally one space, blocking her jump chain.

"So cool," she says after I place the marble into its spot. "Have yet to find anyone else here at least." She breaks her own chain by jumping her piece over mine. "Chances are the next will be in India or China."

I furrow my brow at her. "How did you 'find' me anyway?"

"The incident. Witnesses reported seeing a young boy . . . " She trails off and goes silent for a second before starting again. "How much do you remember of the foster home?"

"Not much on my own." I move a new piece out from my corner and into the center area.

"Well, I wasn't actually directly involved with the Domestic Resources Development Initiative until right around the time of the incident. How's that name? So innocuous. Anyway, it took a couple of weeks to investigate the reports. Then a few more days to screen candidates. Adoption was really fast. Usually, each step would take several times as long, but it was vital that we move to protect you immediately."

"Protect me?"

"Yeah." She moves her forward-most piece sideways one spot, establishing a jump chain across my pieces. "DRDI didn't want to lose track of you until another incident. There were also already rumors of a child with supernatural powers. The plan was to take you to a new location, with a new family, and, well, I think you know the rest by now."

"So, before me Solar Flare spent all its time waiting for something weird to happen?"

"Before you there was no Solar Flare. The Initiative itself had other investigations but nothing that turned up credible evidence: drunk hillbillies seeing Bigfoot, Elvis eating lunch with Jimmy Hoffa, people claiming that weather balloons are UFOs, that kind of tabloid crap. Ben was one of our investigators at the time in fact. He'd follow up on the reports. Of course this all changed after you."

"I'm Solar Flare?"

"Yes and no," she says.

I move a new piece forward once. Dr. Burnett shakes her head.

"What?" I say.

"I'm sorry, I'm just never going to get over how cool that is."

Sessions with Burnett are scheduled on Tuesdays and Thursdays in place of afternoon testing. She's like my alternate class schedule. The sessions typically take less than a third of the time allotted for testing, but the blocks keep time flexible in case I need rest or she can't make it or the talk goes long. She's been warned against meeting me in the common room, but prefers the privacy here over the accessibility of the mess. Only Burnett and Delgado can request that the guards leave the area while I'm here, otherwise they post at the door when I am in the common area, and outside the apartment door when I'm in there. I can invite them into the common room anytime.

Following a Burnett session last week McPherson

and I watched *Iron Man*. He talked about how unrealistic it is to desert combat. Rogers stayed at the door.

Dr. Burnett brings another of her pieces out from her corner.

"You've figured out the tests by now, right? What we're trying to do?"

"You're trying to determine my brain activity while using my abilities," I say.

"That's exactly it."

I take my forward-most piece one spot closer to the empty space in the home corner.

"We want to determine exactly what you're capable of and how it's done." She folds her arms in front of her. "You know that old idea about humans using only ten percent of the brain?" she asks.

"Yeah."

"It's total bullshit." Her eyebrows raise even higher to punctuate her point. "If it were true, then we wouldn't be able to talk. We'd hardly even be able to breathe and walk at the same time."

"I know."

"Of course you do," she says, rolling her eyes in fake irritation. "Please, explain."

I paraphrase an article I read last year when I should be have been studying for Mr. Kaufman's biology class. "The idea came from experiments where rats were run through a maze. Portions of the rats' brains were cut away but the rats were still able to complete the maze. Researches decided those parts of the brain weren't used by the rats and therefore also not by humans."

"Yes," she says, one eyebrow slightly lowered, "because we're the same as rats." She continues, "But there really are certain areas of the brain that we still have no idea about."

She turns in her seat slightly, leaning to one side with one arm on the rest and the other stretching out. She always sat this way in her office. "When you're focusing on manipulating an object your brain activity is primarily in the large cortical and subcortical network, the same sections as those associated with imagination."

I want to correct her here. It's not the object that's being manipulated but the space around the object. Instead I'm that six-year-old again, as indecisive as ever around her. I'm sure she knows it too; it's why she took that position in the chair.

She continues, "However, there is also a great deal of activity in the posterior cingulate cortex." She pauses. "Have you already figured this out?"

I shake my head.

"Huh," she says, actually surprised, "something the brilliant Odin Lewis doesn't know."

"I'm only a minor."

"Well then we'll skip through a lot of the technical mumbo jumbo. The posterior cingulate cortex or," she makes finger quotes, "'dark energy region' actually consumes more energy than any other part of the brain. We know that it's involved in emotional and metabolic functions, but we don't know its role in cognitive ones: knowing, judging, evaluating, reasoning. It's also essential to memory, which makes sense when you're looking into your own past, but not involved in creative or imagination function, like manipulating objects or reading someone else's past. Some activity may be normal but for you, the area lights up like a Christmas tree on fire under a thousand spotlights. It must consume massive amounts of energy, which might explain why you feel tired after extensive use, but nowhere near as exhausted as you should be. Our working theory is that whatever it is that allows you to do what you do somehow draws energy through that region of your brain. Basically, in addition to having the usual functions and capacity open to everyone, you have something extra plugged into your head. A giant battery so to speak. And that might be where your old friend is located."

She moves one of her pieces forward but still in her starting zone.

"Of course, none of this explains why you're able to manifest thoughts into physical reality, but we're learning. There's still a lot we don't know about the brain itself, let alone what an anomaly like yours is capable of. We also don't know if these findings apply to anyone else. You may be completely unique in this respect."

"If only," I mutter.

"What was that?"

"Nothing." I move another piece into position to use the jump chain she left. The dark energy region. Sounds ominously appropriate. That would explain the wave from the inside out that occurs when Wendell laughs, or the way it echoes through every part of my body. Doesn't explain why he's there, how he got there, or anything else. If that's where he is, and that's where my . . . powers . . . come from, does that mean they come from him? When he'd been gone, it was more difficult to see the past and make things happen, but I still could. I doubt he'd tell me, or if even he knows exactly what he is. And he's the one . . . person . . . entity . . . whom I can't look into. The only thing I can never completely know is my own head. That also sounds ominously appropriate.

"So, do you like your new set-up here?" she asks, looking around the room.

"It's all right," is all I say. I don't want to give Delgado anything resembling leverage or validation.

"You must feel like a bird in a cage sometimes. We'll see about getting your parents out here, maybe even your brother. No one else would ever receive security clearance."

"I know."

"How are the tests going?"

I shrug. "Nothing hard. Nice not having to hold back."

"Liberating?" she says. "I imagine it would be like owning a mansion with dozens of rooms and only having a closet to live in."

"Something like that."

"Well, if you feel like being challenged, I'm sure it can be arranged. Winger's been raving endlessly about every little thing. It's all useful data to us," she said. She used the word "us" so that my positive association with her would transfer to Winger and his assistants. "But of course I do not under any circumstances want to ask you to do anything that would compromise your comfort or safety. I hope you know that."

"I do."

"We're eager to learn what you can do and where your limits are—if there are any—but if you feel like something is too taxing, please let me or some of the other scientific staff here know and we'll end the test immediately."

"I understand," I say. I nod toward the board. "Your move."

"Oh." She places her hand just above the board. "You're not psychic, right?"

"Not that I know of."

"Good. I'd hate to think that you're cheating."

"Haven't so far," I say, "but you never know."

Her face lights up. "The best part."

3

PERRY TAPS AT HER COMPUTER TABLET. WHEN PERRY was six she tried to dry the family hamster by placing it in the microwave. Her mother caught her as she was closing the door and slapped Perry hard on the face twice. Hawthorne checks his tablet as he presses the pressure plate. He inspects the support structure securing the plate in place on the test room floor. While Hawthorne was in college, he once used his father's position as a prominent alumnus to force a teacher into raising his grade. Hawthorne nods to Perry across the room when his inspection is done. "Again, please," Perry says.

I feel like a pitcher being scouted by college

teams. Only instead of throwing baseballs with my arm, I'm throwing metal balls roughly the size of baseballs with my mind. So, basically the same thing.

Twenty feet away from me is the force gauge with a skeleton of steel beams angled to channel the impact into the floor. Winger and the others assumed this set up would minimize possible damage to the circuitry laced throughout the room. They have high expectations after the last two days of launching basketballs. Delgado stands rigid against the back wall in the observation room.

Sweat beads on my forehead and under the electrodes. I've lost track of how many throws I've already done. Between forty and fifty, beginning at the low fifties and peaking at eighty-eight miles per hour. The last few have been in the sixty to seventy range. Not bad for chucking a five-pound steel ball through the air, but not the result I or any of them are looking for. Especially not Delgado.

Hawthorne and Perry stand back with their

tablets in both hands. Perry's tablet is plugged into a port in the floor which feeds her multiple camera angles of each throw. A program uses the black grid over the white walls and floor to automatically calculate speed. Hawthorne's tablet routes into the back of the force plate, giving him pressure, location, and dissipation data. Behind the glass, Winger receives all of this and more. Delgado just watches.

I raise the metal ball into place, roughly two feet in front of me. I take a deep breath, picturing the ball as best as I can. Then how I'd like it to take off, the blur it leaves, then the impact. The trouble with imagining motion is in the speed itself. A solid image requires the object to be stationary. I rub at my right bicep once again, although both arms now ache from the repetitive motion of shoving them forward with every throw. The movement isn't necessary, but it helps me visualize the motion. I need all the help I can get. I take two steps and shove my arms out. The ball launches forward.

The ball hits the plate with a loud clank. It drops onto the pad under the gauge. The support structure doesn't notice the impact.

"Eighty-five," Perry says.

Hawthorne checks the calculations on the tablet. Five pounds at eight-five miles an hour, assuming a constant speed, just under ninety-five newtons. Less than half of the force I used to break Kevin's face.

In the room, Winger glances back to Delgado. Delgado does nothing. Winger nods to Hawthorne, who nods to Perry. "Again, please," she says.

I sigh and wipe the sweat from my brow. My arms don't want to move anymore. This is pointless. I peek over to Delgado, his jagged eyes like needles in my skin.

I reposition the ball. I hold it there in front of me. I imagine the ball moving. No, exploding outward, like a cannonball. Not that picturing this has worked so far. Whatever. I take a deep breath and I thrust my arms forward. I groan from the motion.

The ball smacks the plate with a hard thump. The frame remains still. Ball drops to the pad below.

"Ninety-two," Perry says, nodding slightly.

"Highest reading yet," Hawthorne adds.

One hundred and eight point two newtons. Kevin would laugh. What's wrong, he'd say, shot your full load the first time? Can't get it back up? Eric and Dylan would snicker like his comment was something clever.

I tap my chest and see a couple of drops show through the orange uniform. Never been this winded during a test before. Winded for nothing. It's not like I'm gonna break the sound barrier with a goddamn metal ball. I can't even throw harder than a major league pitcher. What's the point of continuing? They've seen what I can do. What more do they want?

Twenty percent, one fifth, of all energy is used by the brain. Burnett said the posterior cingulate cortex, the dark energy region, uses more energy than any other section. The most energized of the most energized. That's in a normal person. For me, that must be like plugging a hundred walk-in freezers into a single electrical outlet. Maybe that's why I feel so . . . cloudy.

"Are you okay, Odin?" Winger asks over the speaker. Delgado glares at him. Winger pauses before he speaks. "Again."

Imagine a catapult. Imagine a grenade launcher. A bungee cord. A bullet. A bullet train. No, like a really fast car. Imagine one of those old pneumatic tube systems that buildings downtown have. Or like a bowling ball knocking down all the pins. I take a breath and shove my arms forward again. Nothing is clear. A drop of sweat flicks from my eyelash.

There's a hard thud followed by a soft squish.

"Eighty-four," says Perry. She stretches her neck back to look into the observation room.

Winger says something to Delgado. "He's spent. This is all we can do today." Delgado replies before angrily yanking the door open to leave. "He's holding back."

I hear, "Are you all right?" Perry is a few paces from her normal position. She leans to whisper to me. "You okay?"

I exhale loudly and wave her away.

"One more time," sighs Winger over the speaker.

Perry and Hawthorne resume their positions. I raise my metal ball.

There's a taste of salt as a sweat droplet falls between my lips. I wipe the back of my hand across my brow. I reset my hands chest-high in front of me. I picture . . . nothing. Nothing at all. Fuck it, whatever. I throw my arms out.

"Seventy-two," says Hawthorne.

"This isn't working," Winger says, leaning over the front console. His shoulders rise and fall with breath. He takes a moment before speaking. "Odin," he looks up at me through the glass as he speaks, "take a break. Get some food. Maybe we'll try something else this afternoon." He motions for the two lab assistants to come in. He slouches into the chair. I wipe the sweat from my head and begin peeling off the electrodes.

Perry leans toward me again. She speaks very quietly, as though the receivers everywhere may not pick up the sound. "Get some rest," she says before sliding away.

I wait until they're both gone before dropping to the ground.

The inside of my uniform is damp, especially around the neck and under the arms. It's been a long time since I've been this sweaty. Probably not since my last P.E. test. The lab door hums as it opens and I hear McPherson and Rogers snap to attention on either side of the exit. I probably reek, but I'm sure they've both endured much worse.

The air is cooler outside and without the

stagnant quality of the testing room. I let my head fall back as I exhale. I lean against the door after it closes behind me. It's almost comforting how sterile and bright the bare white walls are. The lights, the cameras, the coded signs of PJSLFR142-01 N03 (North 03, I assume), in their precisely designated place. Even my armed escorts are exactly where they are supposed to be, flanking me in case I decide to cause trouble and have to be eliminated. Never thought it would be such a relief to be back among the guys with the guns.

"Everything all right?" McPherson asks, a slight frown of either genuine or very well practiced concern.

"Yeah . . . just tired."

"You look tired," he says. "What was it today?"

"Force testing," I say. I use the bottom of my shirt to wipe my brow. "Hurling balls at a pressure gauge. Steel balls. Five pounds."

"You can do that?"

"Not well."

"Is that why you're tired?" he asks.

"Not sure. I can't, like . . . " I pause. It's mental fatigue. More than usual. Like wading through hours of a complex science text that you simply don't understand. That's what I want to say. "Can't get . . . " That's not what I meant. "Like, my head to work. Not right."

There's a metallic snap as Roger's steadies his gun. A blur of McPherson waving him down.

"You need to see the medic?" McPherson asks.

"No," I say, "just want a second to rest." I slide against the door behind me until I'm sitting on the cold, clean floor. The surface is smoother than paper. It's almost plastic. Does the camera above the door see me down here? I know those at the corners of the room do. I see Rogers lower his gun. I gather my words before speaking again.

"Could you guys kinda let me stay here by myself a minute?"

"That's not possible," says McPherson flatly.

"I just want to sit here a little while and then get

food." I look up and around McPherson to the square room with nothing in it but doors and cameras to watch all who enter those doors. Behind me is the one door I'm allowed to enter alone, to the right is one none of us can enter, and across from me is the elevator door we soon plan to enter. "I'm going to head up to mess in a couple minutes," I say, gesturing weakly toward the opposite wall, "I can meet you there."

"That's not possible," McPherson says. There's silence for a moment, then I hear their gear shake with motion. "But," McPherson says, "we can let you stay here while we wait for the elevator."

I nod. "Thanks."

McPherson rattles as he steps away. I feel a weight on my shoulder.

"Hang in there, kid," says Rogers.

Today's menu: meat spaghetti with a side salad of mostly iceberg lettuce and carrots, the daily fixture of hamburger and fries, or a vegetarian chili that's basically beans and carrots and more beans. The four cooks that rotate between meal shifts are all Army food service specialists reassigned to Project Solar Flare. They were chosen less for their cooking skills than their willingness to not ask questions. The only time all four are present is during food delivery every Wednesday at eleven, after lights-out and just before complete lockdown of the complex at midnight.

Originally the head food service specialist, Nelson Burns, wanted to use this assignment to grow toward his eventual goal of becoming a sous chef for a restaurant back home in Charlotte. After the requisitions officer guffawed at his requests for duck, broccoli rabe, pork shoulder, and cumin and returned with several pounds of ground beef, carrots, ground pork, and no seasoning, Burns gave up trying anything new or interesting. He made a menu for that week from what he had and has used the same weekly menu ever since. After all, he was assigned here to cook, not to ask questions. By Tuesday morning most of what's left gets thrown together into a pot. Hence: meat spaghetti, standard hamburger and fries, and vegetarian chili.

"This is so much better than what they serve in the barracks," McPherson says between burger bites.

Rogers nods emphatically as he chews. He pauses long enough to mutter, "Or MREs," from the side of his mouth before swallowing.

"The beef stew wasn't bad. Of course it's kinda hard to screw up beef stew."

Rogers laughs. A bit of burger hangs on the stubble on his upper lip.

We sit at the exact center table in the mess area. Two other groups occupy extremes of the dozen tables arranged in a four-by-three grid. Typically, McPherson and Rogers stand against the wall next to the exit from the main passage while I eat both breakfast and lunch. Today, for some reason, they decided to sit and have a bite. They sit with their guns pushed onto their backs. It was their idea to sit in the middle of the room. I wanted to linger just inside the door.

The other groups are two technicians on my left and two lab assistants, a researcher, and a technician on my right. The two lab assistants were by themselves at that same table yesterday. The technicians were there a couple of days ago, with a third, also at that same table. Funny, they could sit anywhere with anyone else but sit in the same place with the same people. Some conditioning never changes. One in the party of two glances at me over his shoulder. He looks away and whispers to the other. Yup, never changes.

They ate pizza last night, Ben, Aida, and Andre. Ben and Aida sat on the couch while Andre was between them on the floor. They watched a movie while eating. Andre picked off the mushrooms and Dad added them to his own slice. He said he likes "fungi" because he's a "fun guy." Mom and Andre rolled their eyes.

They told Andre that I had accepted an earlier acceptance to a university in Chicago which required that I start a summer class immediately. He asked if they would visit me. They said they'll try. They haven't talked about it since then. They closed the door to my room when they got home after picking up Andre from the Aukermans the night I arrived here. Aida has since gone into my room once to clean. That's all. Life goes on without me.

"In Afghanistan we had this cook," Rogers pauses in memory, "Sanchez or something like that, who would take all the meat from the rations, if it was stew or spaghetti or whatever it was, chop it all up, cook it all in a pot, and then would actually hand roll about two hundred tortillas and make burritos for everyone."

"Really?" McPherson says, burger clutched up in one hand.

"No foolin', full burritos." Rogers places his

hands out as though holding a cylinder. "Rolled up and everything, like a pipe bomb."

McPherson shakes his head in awe.

"Course then I got redeployed to Iraq and it was nothing but those muffins and energy bars. All the pre-packed stuff with the labels on it. Like they need to advertise to us."

"Right? We actually had a Burger King truck come by regularly with a big logo on the side. Imagine having to drive that thing from town out to the camp."

There were about twenty soldiers at Camp Arrow in Ad-Dawr whom McPherson would regularly play football with while not on patrol. Although he preferred being on defense, he had his best plays at running back. There was one instance in particular, a sweep left. His lead blocker tripped and the hole closed. He had to circle to the other side of the field. He turned the corner with only one other guy to beat, did a spin move that kicked sand out like a fishtail, and sprinted into the end zone. One blocker asked why he did that, they had a hole for him. He told one of them that the only hole he saw was the one the blocker was lying in after he fell down. That blocker, a reservist named Blankenship, died from an improvised explosive device three months later.

Rogers became friends with the soldier in the hospital bed next to him during his recovery at Walter Reed. The other patient, Private David Larsen, had suffered burns and shrapnel injuries from a roadside mortar attack outside of Mosul. He spent most of Rogers' time there with bandages covering half of his face and most of his right arm. Rogers would sit on his bed and pretend to be a mummy coming to recruit Larsen to their cause. "You're already halfway there," he'd say, "join us." Larsen said he'd have laughed, but the stretching of his face hurt too much. They kept in touch through email for a few months after Rogers left. In one message Larsen wrote about how the corrective surgery on his face gave him a plastic look and made him feel like a toy. Toy soldier, he called himself. Easily manipulated and easily replaced. Rogers didn't write back after that. He did a Google search last year to see that Private David Larsen, resident of Springfield, Illinois, was found dead of a codeine overdose two years after that last letter.

"What's it like?" I hear from across the table. I look up to see McPherson staring at me. "What's it look like?"

"What?"

"The floaty thing you can do."

"It's just something floating. Like it's falling but doesn't move."

"Can you do it now?"

He looks eager, Rogers too, school children waiting for the teacher to decide which storybook to read that day.

"Yeah. But I was told not to outside of the lab."

"C'mon, I gotta see it once," says McPherson.

"I was told that any use of my . . . abilities . . . outside of the lab would be considered a threat."

"I'm not going shoot you. Are you gonna shoot him?" McPherson points to Rogers.

"Not without reason."

"See? So, c'mon, just a little thing."

"All right," I say. I place my fork onto the table between all of us. I put my hand over it. I don't picture anything. The fork lifts from the table five inches and hovers there.

"Holy shit!" yells McPherson, throwing his hands onto his head. "That's really floating there!"

"It's pretty simple actually."

Rogers says nothing, but his eyes are tablespoons and his face is slack.

"That's the coolest thing I've ever seen in my life," McPherson says.

"First thing I learned to do," I say.

"It's still the coolest thing I've ever seen in my life."

Looking up, I see almost every other eye in the room focused on the fork between the three of us.

I nod. "Yeah, it is pretty cool."

***

The idea was that a more responsive experience would yield better results. Thus, the afternoon's examination replaced the metal framework with a table and metal backboard against the wall and the pressure plate with a one-inch concrete slab. A tactile response would propel the subject—that's what Winger calls me among his colleagues, "the subject"—to work harder. As though I wasn't already working the hardest I could without literally bashing my head against the wall.

I groan as I once again launch this annoying metal ball at yet another target. Same action, different reaction. Hawthorne puts his hand out to check if there is any damage to the block. Perry watches the camera feed through the safety goggles they both wear. Hawthorne shakes his head and motions for another throw. Another groan. My arms burn.

This is pathetic.

I try to keep my lips from moving as I speak. "Quiet," I whisper.

I stop the ball from rolling around on the table. Hawthorne wipes a gloved hand over the surface of the block. He shakes his head. Winger inside the observation room sighs. Delgado does nothing.

Stop holding back.

"I'm not," I say before remembering the whole place is wired for sound. They don't seem to have heard me. Not yet at least.

I raise the ball again, more out of habit than anything else. This is what I do now. I pointlessly throw objects at other objects. Everything that came before has been building up to this moment. There is nothing more. I set my hands in front of me to reposition the ball. I make no great effort in pushing away. My arms ache with every movement.

I'm in the cool-down at the end of a long workout. Doing the motions because it's what I need to do, but any benefit is long past.

"Fifty-eight," says Perry. She has about as much interest in that number I as do.

You are.

I swing around to face Winger through the glass. My arms hang from slumped shoulders. I breathe heavily and feel the sweat pooling around the electrode connections.

"Odin," Winger says.

You know you are.

"Is something wrong?"

Delgado cocks his head.

Stop thinking. Just do.

"This is not possible," I say loudly.

Winger blinks idly.

"A five-pound object at fifty-eight miles per hour for a total of," I search for the calculation, "sixty-four point eight two newtons. Meanwhile these slabs can withstand," I look for the information, an article I read years ago on the physics of Karate masters breaking objects with their bare hands, "Nineteen-hundred newtons. That would require more than," calculation again, "Seventeen-hundred miles per hour." I pause for emphasis. "It's not physically possible."

That makes no difference.

"Odin," Winger says. Then he stops and releases the speaker button. He takes a breath before continuing. "None of this is physically possible. I don't think that should stop us now."

"The physics don't even work," I argue back.

That means nothing.

"Neither does changing the flight of an object in midair," Winger argues. Delgado tilts his head the other way.

"That's not the same!" I lurch forward as I speak, feeling beads of sweat fly from my forehead. "You're asking me to create energy. That's not possible."

"Odin," says Winger, trying to be calming. "You're already doing that. We just want to see exactly what you're capable of."

"Congratulations! You found it! I am incapable of generating physically impossible levels of force. Maybe they'll give you goddamn medal!"

Delgado rises his chin and puffs his chest out.

"Odin—"

It is no matter for you.

I look at Delgado instead. His chin points at me like an accusation. "You're asking me to create energy equal to a fucking cannon!" I'm not angry. I'm tired. "It isn't physically fucking possible!"

Stop holding back.

I want to lie down, sleep, and forget this day ever happened. I want to wake up in my room, *my* room, with my computer and books and the old toys that I haven't played with in years but can't make myself get rid of. Hell, I'd play with them all day right now if I could. I want to pick up my phone to see a message from Evelyn just saying hi and asking how my day is.

"What's the point of this anyway?" I yell at the general. I grab the two wires running behind my ear and yank at them. The electrodes pull tightly on the front and back of my head but pop off. What's the worst he can do? Take away my fancy room with the TV and the books I rarely get to use? They're not mine anyway. None of this is. If I'm going to be a prisoner, I'd rather see the damn bars. Delgado doesn't respond.

"Why," I say at last, "are you doing this to me?"

I'm not. You are.

Winger leans onto the console to make eye contact with his assistants. He motions for both of them to exit the test room.

"Yeah. Run," I say. "Run from the monster." I look directly at Winger. "The subject."

Winger freezes. Perry presses her fingers into the pad next to the observation side door.

I scratch another of the electrodes away, feeling my nails dig against my scalp. I take two steps closer to the glass, pulling off the last two wires one by one. "Run," I say again.

"Odin," Winger finally says. "I understand today's been very stressful. We'll stop here."

I walk right up in front of him, the closest we've ever come to being face to face. He's older than I thought, with faint lines stemming from the corners of his eyes and little white hairs mixed in his beard. I see his head shaking in fear. I step to the side to face Delgado head on.

"No guards with you in there," I say. I tap the glass. It makes a hollow sound. "Not as thick as concrete. And then, what's left?"

He keeps his hands behind his back. He lowers his chin. The cracks in his face seem to deepen.

Pathetic.

Winger reaches for the button.

"We're done for today, Odin," he says. "Get some rest."

Delgado spins on his heels and yanks the door open. I hear it slam closed from out here.

"Things will be different tomorrow," Winger says. "Promise."

I turn and walk heavily toward the door. Harris and Carter wait outside to escort me back to my room, "my" room, with the bolted down bed and table and absolutely nothing that was ever or will ever be *mine*. The place they allowed me to have for being such a good little subject. The place where I'm contained.

"You," I move my lips as little as possible, so they won't see me talking to myself, "are not welcome."

That was stupid.

Another stupid thing that I did for no damn reason.

The same thinking that got me stuck in this place with these people.

I turn the knob and push my door open. "Let us know if you need anything," Carter says from over my shoulder.

"Yeah," says Harris on the other side. "Not like we won't be here." He's trying to be funny. He shouldn't. I close the door behind me.

Why are you doing this?

"Just shut up." I walk directly into the bathroom.

Why do you still allow yourself to be so limited?

I splash two handfuls of water on my face. The sweat is already drying everywhere. I duck into the sink and pour water onto my head. I sway to feel the water run down every side. Another nice thing about not having any hair. I straighten up and reach for the towel hanging next to the door. Fresh towels. Every day. I'm just so goddamn privileged.

After all the limits placed on you during your previous life—

"Is that what you call it?" I stare into the polished metal as though having a conversation with myself, which I technically am.

All the limits placed on you there. You should embrace the chance to excel.

"You sound like him," I say, looking at myself. My eyes look almost yellow. Possibly from fatigue, or anger, or maybe they look this way when I'm talking to the voice in my head. I don't know. "Like this program is some reward I should be proud for. I didn't ask for this, and I don't fucking care about it."

You should. This is your opportunity.

"Opportunity for what?" I yell at myself.

To become what you are meant to become.

I toss the towel on floor.

Instead you allow yourself to be limited.

I make a face into the metal as though growling. "Is this what you want me to be? Or what they want me to be? What about what I want? Doesn't that mean shit to anyone in this world?"

No. That is not your choice.

I yell. I slam my hand against the metal plate bolted to the wall. The sound vibrates loudly around the bathroom. I freeze when I think the guards outside might've heard me. Don't know how thick the walls are. No response.

I step out of the bathroom. I walk between the bed, table, and bathroom door. "Why not?" I say more quietly. "What's stopping me? I thought I could do anything."

You can.

I pause in the center of the room, waiting for him to continue. "Well," I say when I tire of waiting. "Do you see how that's a contradiction?"

As long as you allow yourself to be limited, you will never be more than they wish you to be.

"Limited by what?"

By your world.

"How does the world limit me?"

By your understanding of your world.

"By physical reality, you mean?" I scoff. "By nature and science and all the things that keep the Earth spinning and us from falling off of it. You sound like Winger."

They are not wrong. The physical limits of this world are not a concern for you.

"No shit?" I say. "I figured that part already, but apparently breaking all of Newton's laws of motion aren't enough." I look across the room as though looking for something else to break. Of course there isn't anything. That's the point of this room. "Now I have to fire fucking cannonballs with my brain or it's a waste of everyone's time and investment and promise to the whole fucking country." I shake my head. "I shouldn't have said anything to him. That was so stupid."

You are limiting yourself by what you believe to be possible.

"I'm already doing impossible things!" My voice raises again.

That is not enough.

I slouch against the bed. I place both hands and pull my head down to stretch my neck.

"They're going to kill me here."

No. Not yet. Not while you are still valuable.

I stifle a laugh. "That's reassuring. Thanks."

You must use them as they are using you. Learn all you can. Teach yourself.

I extend one arm and then the other. Try to bend my elbows backward to stretch the biceps. It doesn't work.

Do not focus on how to make reality work. Make it work.

I push my shoulders back. It's nice to be able to move without pain in my ribs. I look down at my hands. The scars from the glass in Hauser's windows blend with the lines in my palms. Leftovers from my previous life.

"That doesn't make any sense," I say.

As long as you believe that, you will never be able to escape.

"Now *that* is something that is not a choice."

Then you will always be a prisoner. Here or anywhere. You will never be free.

4

IT'S EIGHT O'CLOCK, TIME TO FACE THE CONSEQUENCES.
McPherson and Rogers take their positions
on either side of the lab room door. I look up at
the camera atop the entrance. Whoever is inside
the central security room now decides whether or
not I get to enter. There's a low hum as the door
opens. I look over to McPherson, who is staring
straight ahead, then to Rogers, who is equally
expressionless. I keep my head down as I step in.

Dr. Burnett sits in one of the two chairs facing
each other in the middle of the gridded room.
Metal chairs, like those found in a shopping mall
food court, and nothing else.

"Good morning, Odin," she says in a tone that is simultaneously pleasant and authoritative. A tone that only doctors seem to have perfected. "I hope you slept well." She gestures for me to sit. "Please," she says.

I check my surroundings like someone might appear out of nowhere at any moment.

"Not what you were expecting today?" she says. She crosses her legs and folds her hands into her lap. "I'd tell you to get used to things not being what you expect, but I can't imagine you don't already know that." I make sure there's nothing on the seat or the armrests before sitting.

The lab room looks cavernous with only the two of us in here in our small chairs. No targets at the end, no objects to throw, no assistants, no wires, nothing. Fifty feet of empty white walls and floors, black lines drawn every five feet, ten down, five across, dividing the room into little squares. Squares in a rectangle in a box, neat and clean and tidy, everything in its specific place. Including me.

"Would you like to talk about yesterday's examinations?"

I tilt my head and look at her, the lines under her eyes are from age, the dark circles starting to form aren't. "Not really."

"Well, I would."

I shrug.

"I understand that you became quite frustrated yesterday and that frustration might've lead you to be less . . . we'll say cooperative . . . than you'd otherwise be."

"You could say that," I mutter.

"The frustration is understandable," she says. I can feel her eyes sticking on me like those in a portrait on the wall of an art museum. "You're in this strange place—" She looks around the room for a second. The interior looks like it belongs on the wall of a totally different art museum. "—doing strange things, with no explanation as to why you should do any of it. You could find those answers but you haven't. You've been quite trusting and we, I, appreciate that very much."

She's speaking in the way she does when she's being watched. "How do you know I haven't?"

"Because yesterday you asked why we are doing this. It's my belief that if you knew why, you wouldn't become frustrated. Instead, you'd find it very interesting."

I look away, shake my head. "Or it's because you conditioned me not to seek answers for myself," I say.

"That's always a possibility," she replies.

"Of course," I nod as though I knew she'd respond that way. "Anything is possible."

She considers her words for a moment. "Isn't that why we're here? Possibility?" It's her turn to look around as though a surprise were about to spring out. "We're in a box," she says. "Theoretically no one outside knows if we're still alive in this box."

"Except for the people watching the cameras," I say.

"Go with me here, Odin, I'm trying to help," she replies in quick, dry tone.

I lean back. The chair creaks under me as though it were old, or made of old parts.

"For those outside, we continue in this limbo state between living and dead until we finally offer them proof that we're alive," she says. "Or until the people watching the cameras tell them."

She's talking about the Schrodinger's cat experiment. "Two possible worlds," I say, "one where we live and one where we die."

"Why are those the only worlds? What about worlds where we never entered the box? Worlds where the box itself doesn't exist. Those are also possibilities."

I narrow my eyes at her. Where is she going with this?

"In this way," she says, "anything is possible. And we're seeing that through everything you've been able to do here."

"Well, I'm thrilled to know that I'm your proof of concept."

"You're more than that, Odin. You always have been. You're the key to unlocking so many things we've never understood about the universe. Not just the theoretical side, but on the practical side. The infinite possibilities open to us outside the box." She pauses, then says, "I'm sorry, the pun was unavoidable."

"But what they're asking me to do," I say, "is physically impossible." I lean forward. The chair squeaks again. "There are limits. Physical limits." He's not here, not right now, but I still hear Wendell's voice from last night asking why I allow myself to be limited. "That's how the world works."

"So?" she says. "You break physical limits all the time."

"Easy things. Picking up a book and turning it and opening it. That's nothing."

She cocks her head at me.

"Well . . . not nothing, but it's . . . easy. I can

picture and see it and understand it. This breaking concrete blocks with metal balls thing they made me do, it doesn't make any sense." I lean even farther forward. The chair creaks like the joints of the front legs could break at any second. "The physics of it don't work."

She gestures as though she's presenting me with a gift.

"I can imagine the movement, but the amount of force that's generated . . . I can't get a solid image of the movement needed and still make it move. It's like taking a photograph of movement. The photograph is one frozen moment in the movement. The image itself makes the movement stop."

"Maybe you don't have to," she says. "Maybe it's like the rest of the world. You set the change in motion and it just happens."

"That's not how it works with me." I imagine Wendell speaking again: *Do not focus on how to make reality work. Make it work.*

"How do you know?" she asks.

"Because that's not how it worked in the past."
My fight with Kevin. I pictured my bag floating in
the air. I threw it exactly as I imagined.

"Odin," she says with a slight smile. "If we
always do what we did in the past then we'd still
rub stick together to make fire."

My eyes narrow at her.

"What I mean to say is, you're already changing
the entire way the physical world operates. You're
making the impossible possible. So why is the concept of other possibilities so difficult?"

I didn't picture how or why my backpack was able
to move during the fight with Kevin. Not even its
precise speed or target. I didn't think of how to stop
David's second punch or how to break Eric's arm.

I just make them happen. I made it work.

"You're a smart kid, Odin." There's that phrase
again. "And yes, we did . . . program you . . . to
have feelings of trust and guilt toward obtaining
information we didn't want you to have. But one
way or another you've always been able to figure

things out for yourself. Because of this it can be extremely frustrating when something doesn't appear to make sense. I was the same way at your age." She bounces her head slightly side to side. "Minus the programming and the power."

"That sounds about right."

"Well, okay," she says, nodding decisively. "Let's help alleviate some of that frustration right now." She unfolds her legs and pushes up from the chair. "Follow me," she says.

"What's happening?" I say while standing.

"I'm going to show you why we're doing this." Dr. Burnett walks over to the observation side door. She scans her fingerprints into the screen. "I'm sure you'll find it very interesting." She motions for me to walk through the door after her. I'd been told during my first test session that if I was caught behind that door, I would be treated as hostile.

She sees me hesitate. "Right," she says, "I am authorized to enter this area and hereby authorize you to do the same. So, c'mon. Let's help you understand."

The door leads into a narrow passageway. The table and the concrete blocks, the metal structure with the pressure gauge, the basketball hoop, and other items I recognize from previous testing sessions clutter against the left wall. The wall to my right appears to extend behind the observation room in the testing lab. The passage ends in an automatic door, like a supermarket entrance, which opens the moment Burnett steps within three feet.

The path forward is as wide as the testing room is long. I can't even see the end of this area from here, only piles of scrap materials and dozens of workstations leading down a long hall. The ceiling is obscured by a mass of hanging lights and exposed pipes crisscrossing openly. There are none of the embedded and molded textures of the rest of the complex. The gathered materials lining the walls make a space for the countless doors which open and close as lab technicians traverse the room. The doors have handles. Regular handles. No touch screens or intricate locks here.

I follow Burnett forward. A half a dozen men in gray jumpsuits and welding masks work with blowtorches on a metal cylinder that is taller than they are. A large and reinforced saw is pushed off to the side and locked in place. One of the workers lifts his welding mask as we pass. He points us out to another of the workers.

"That's him?" one of them says.

"I dunno," says the other.

The clutter along the walls looks like the stuff left at the city dump after trash day. Metal pipes with jagged ends, old office chairs with the wheels missing and the cushions ripped off, folding tables with the legs removed, old computer monitors with the glass and wiring stripped out, and what looks like high school lockers but without the doors or the back or anything inside, just a sequence of metal rectangles pushed against a wall.

Through the windows I can see the labs behind the doors. Feels like forever since I'd seen a window that didn't have Winger and Delgado behind it.

Technicians like those I'd seen in the mess hall holler to each other from behind computer terminals. They point at their screens for others to see, sip coffee from styrofoam cups, and slap printers to make them work. I catch eyes with one female technician glancing up from her computer. She leans quickly to follow me before I disappear behind the wall between us.

No glass covers the cameras above us. The floor here is scratched and scuffed, like that of the school. Drains are placed regularly across the floor under every fixed work station. I follow Burnett along a path between the cluttered scrap against the side and the series of workstations in the middle of the room. We're far beyond the sloping piles of old metal bars and arcade game boxes with the interiors torn out and the workers' flying sparks and trails of leaking oil.

Another group of workers take turns pounding hammers against a long coil of braided metal. There's the sound of grinders, belt sanders, drills, electric saws, and more hammers. On the far side of the room a yellow forklift rolls into the distance.

We continue on until the room starts to feel familiar. The passage from the testing lab is barely visible behind me, and the end of the fabrication area is still far ahead. It's as though we stepped into a construction site limbo that's building itself to stretch to eternity. Then I see a long window high on the far wall. It overlooks a huge, lifting door on the other side. I've seen this before. During my first day here. It's the camera room up there, the place where Ben and Aida were when they spoke to me. The place with the screens that watch us all, even those in the box. I wonder if the same guards are up there now who were there my first night here, the ones who cleared out for my parents, handlers, to speak with me. Who watched me pace around in that tiny cell, ripping apart a uniform identical to the one I now wear, lick my plate of mushy brown "food" clean, pound my hands bloody against the walls, and curse at them through the camera as they watched. The same guards who saw me strip off the blood-stained clothes I was marched into this place in and curl up to cry every night in the hole where Delgado stuck me. They still watch me today, in that big common room. No matter where I go, I can't escape them. *They*, that room, are always watching.

"Are you starting to understand?" Burnett says, once the noise of construction is well behind us.

"I understand that this is where testing equipment is put together," I reply.

"Yes," she says, "that's part of it. A very, very small part of it."

Finally, after what feels like a mostly silent hour but was probably just several minutes, the end comes into view. The rear wall has another of the huge, lifting doors in it, almost as wide as the room and half as tall. As we approach, I see that it's a freight elevator with tire and scruff marks leading right up to the very bottom of the door. Burnett lightly presses the big, red button in the corner. She appears to rub away some dirt from her fingertip. There's a heavy rumble when the door rises as one solid plate toward the ceiling. A thinner, interior gate lifts as well, rolling upward like a garage door, a garage large enough to house cement trucks and construction cranes. Scrapes, tracks, and grease litter the floor. The back wall is another interior gate, exactly the same as the one curved above us. Burnett motions for me to enter.

Inside, Burnett presses another button on the interior wall and the two doors slowly lower. It all feels somewhat excessive, a giant freight elevator with only us inside. So much effort put into transporting two people just to make a point. The elevator starts to move, not down, but forward. It's more like a mining car than an elevator. There's a sound like a bus putting on its brakes.

"So far it appears our theories about you have been correct." Burnett says loudly. "The brain scans have been remarkably consistent with what was expected years ago, when we first learned of your existence."

She steps away and places her hand against the elevator wall. She balances to check the bottom of her shoe. Her lip curls as she says something I can't hear over the elevator noise. Then she quickly removes her hand from the wall and looks at it. I can hear her, "Aw, shit." She looks around for something to wipe it onto before giving up.

"As we talked about before," she says, keeping the grease-stained hand a bit away from the rest of her, "we've long suspected that your brain is wired in a way differently than anyone else's. This wiring allows the PCC to be exponentially more active than normal." She glances at her hand again. The dirt looks like she just finished making one of the finger paintings that used to adorn her office door.

"The working theory," she continues, "is that whatever this energy source is that's plugged into your brain allows your imagination to affect reality." She moves her hands in the air in front of her as though shaping a clay pot. "This would be why you're able to create and destroy energy from seemingly nothing, which is of course totally against the laws of physics." She claps her hands together. Her eyes close and her head drops. "Oh, goddammit," she says quietly. I can't help but chuckle when she sees the grease has spread between both hands.

"I'd offer you my sleeve," I say, "but these clothes are government property."

"Yeah," she mutters, "laugh it up, brain boy."

I try not to.

"Anyway," she says, putting both hands down and away from her, "throwing objects, spinning them, stopping and turning them in mid-flight without using any outside force breaks one of the most fundamental principles—"

"Conservation of energy," I say. The answer to number twenty-three on Mr. Zeller's exam.

"Exactly right," Burnett says, pointing quickly. I feel the car begin to slow. "And these are things we've seen you do every day."

There are squeaks and a rumble as the transport

comes to a stop. The lifting door shakes the entire car like an earthquake.

"So it's hard for me to understand why you find it impossible to do something when everything you do is impossible."

Outside of our transport is a hangar, easily as big as the one where Choi handed me over to Delgado. It runs into the dark distance, a more massive underground structure than I've ever imagined. Are we still under the base?

There's motion in every direction in front of us. Hundreds of people throw shadows in every direction as lights line the walls and hang from the ceiling. Crane hooks extend high above us from construction vehicles on the floor. Metal shipping crates are stacked three-high on both sides. There are trucks, forklifts, carts, wheeled staircases, and several dozen workers wearing hard hats and tool belts.

"C'mon." Burnett motions for me to move on, into the commotion of construction. She walks fast, weaving around men pushing what appears to be hundreds of miles of thin wiring.

And in the middle of everything, the massive space and all the activity contained within it, is a round, metal tunnel twice as tall as the three men I see walking into it.

The outside shell is a slightly green hue, like an old, gigantic sewer pipe. The inside is shining metal, light blue blending to gleaming copper. Perfectly symmetrical. Eight straight lines running down the length of the rounded interior with a set of stairs at the front and handrails the only way to distinguish bottom from top. Internal divisions segment the tunnel, as though each part could spin independently of the others, reconnecting in a new formation.

I notice that I've stopped moving. Burnett motions for us to continue. "This is what you're here for, Odin," she says, an air of purpose and pride in her voice, "and this is here because of you."

"What is it?"

91

"This is Solar Flare. The actual Solar Flare."

"I thought I was . . . " I let the thought die as we approach the mouth of the metal tunnel.

"You are, in a way. This project wouldn't be possible without you. Excuse me." Dr. Burnett approaches one of the workers near the entrance of the tunnel. He sees her, then me, and looks around like a kid who didn't do the homework being called to answer a question. She points at the dirty rag hanging from his tool belt. "Not great," she says, after wiping her hands, "but better." She motions for me to follow her to the stairs leading into the entrance of the gaping machine. I hear a few whispers from the workers behind us.

I see a thousand little versions of myself in the panels lining the interior walls, standing out in my bright orange uniform. There's a breeze, the dull echo of the men further down the tunnel, and a faint smell of rubbing alcohol. Each panel tilts inward, layered like scales on a lizard's back, with tiny motors barely visible. Long pipes, horizontal and spaced evenly around, begin and end at the segment, with a series of wires or tubes running from under them to somewhere between the polished panels. In operation, I imagine, the effect would be like combining the Gravitron carnival ride with the hall of mirrors, if it's even possible to be in here during operation.

I reach out to see my hand reflected back in one panel and from a thousand angles in a thousand others. "Don't!" she says, seeing me without seeing me, echoing from a thousand directions. "It's . . . delicate," she says more quietly.

"So what exactly is this thing?" I ask. "Other than Solar Flare, the reason we're here, and because of me."

Burnett turns; I see the motion everywhere. She gestures for me to move back to the exit. "Basically," she says as we move down the steps, "this is a brain. Any brain, really, but specifically your brain. Or it will be when it's completed."

I watch as she takes her last step down. "So you're saying my brain is empty."

She smiles kindly, a hint of fatigue setting in. "Of course not, and neither is this machine. See the outer rim here?" She points to the thick layer of greenish metal encircling the hollow center of the machine. "Inside of there are thousands of miles of wires forming millions of direct electrical connections and billions of indirect connections through every inch of this entire structure." She leads me around the side of the pipe-like construct. We avoid a pair of workers descending a set of mobile stairs and step over big bundles of chords extending from the bottom of the machine into holes in the hangar walls. The machine continues on for a hundred feet, maybe more. "Impressive, isn't it? And all of this to simulate one human brain."

"Yeah," I say, nodding. "I have an impressive, big, empty brain."

Eyebrows up. "Smartass."

"One of those, too."

She continues on ahead. I crane my neck around

to see around the crates and equipment, the flurry of workers, some stopping to stare. They slap each other on the arm and point as we pass. The tunnel continues well beyond the end of the machine.

"Isn't that what a computer does?" I ask.

"This isn't to simulate the process of accessing information." We keep moving. Massive ducts descend from the darkness of the ceiling. "It's to simulate the actual electrical currents at work in your brain."

The other end of the machine is sealed with a rounded cap like the front end of a nuclear submarine. More crates with building equipment stretch toward another freight transport on the wall opposite where we stand. In the distance, the hangar ends with a wall divided in half by a single thick line, not unlike the front door to the complex that Delgado marched me through, but much, much larger. This underground structure must be so much bigger than the complex I know. Multiple entrances and exits for personnel and equipment.

Where are we now anyway? We can't be under the base.

On the wall next to us is an opened metal door with a wheel-like steering handle. Similar doors are spaced all along both walls, the type of doors used to create an airtight barrier. Are we so far north that the lake reaches us? Burnett motions for me to enter the hallway behind that door.

It's well lit, similar to the halls in the complex but without the white walls and molded features. There's a thickness to the air, a faint buzz in the background. I feel the thin hairs on my forearms pulling upward. The buzz gets louder, joining a mechanical hum and, gradually, a couple of human voices.

Another open door leads to a computer lab with large databanks and gauges and a dozen more technicians or scientists, I can't tell which they are, checking connections and monitors. One in particular gestures wildly while speaking with another. Burnett approaches but puts a hand up in front of me in silence. The man with salt-and-pepper hair and a slight slouch in his shoulders finally stops talking.

"Excuse me," Burnett says.

The man sighs.

"Dr. Sarsgaard?"

He turns. He's maybe in his fifties, with small blue eyes and a large nose angled downward, an arrow in the middle of his face.

"I'm Dr. Alice Burnett and this is Odin. Odin Lewis."

Sarsgaard shakes his head. "Yes?"

"I thought you might like to explain to Odin what you're doing here. What you're doing with *his* brain wave patterns."

Sarsgaard stands upright and takes his time looking around the room.

"Did Delgado send you down here?"

"No," says Burnett, a degree of offense and confusion in her tone. "But I am authorized."

"Then I imagine you are also authorized to

explain to the"—he glances over at me—"boy, the nature of our experiment rather than asking me to start from the beginning when we need to push toward the end."

Burnett says nothing. I also say nothing.

"Well?"

"Thank you for your time," Burnett says. Sarsgaard looks away. He charges over to where another tech is tapping the glass over a gauge. "Dr. Jackass," Burnett whispers as she walks past me. We walk toward the sound of construction once again, drowning out: "Dr. Sarsgaard, that was . . ." from within the computer room.

"That ass," Burnett mutters as we exit the tunnel, "even with degrees in child psychology, neurology, abnormal psychology . . . " she glances up to the massive machine, " . . . still not . . . " she huffs. We walk back toward the opposite end, the direction of the transport from the complex. She stops to take a breath. "I'd hoped that Dr. Sarsgaard wouldn't live up to his reputation as a pathological asshole, but apparently—" She takes a moment before starting again. "Remember the posterior cingulate cortex we talked—of course you do." She closes her eyes and presses her fingers to her forehead. "Nothing is ever easy," she mutters, "nothing is ever fucking easy." She drops her hand and opens her eyes with one quick motion. "The best way I can explain it is that this machine is made to mimic the electrical sequence that occurs in your brain when using your abilities." She looks at me. "You've figured this part out already, haven't you?"

"Pretty much."

She sighs. "Okay, let's see what you know. Tell me how this machine works."

"Hmmm—"

"Not the internal structure and construction, and *not* by looking into anyone else's memory. Let's see you use that impressive, big, empty brain of yours."

"Okay," I start as we walk, ignoring the urge to lift every answer directly from the source. "By recreating my brain wave pattern, you hope to access the same energy source that I do."

"Exactly," she interrupts with a confident nod. "Unlimited, renewable energy forever. No more fossil fuels, no more nuclear waste, no more pollution or greenhouse gases, no more climate change. It's still technically a theory until proven, but even gravity and evolution are still considered theories, and those are pretty definitive."

"But where does that energy come from?"

We pass a trio of workers who scoot out of our way as we approach. "This is again outside of my particular field. Frankly, quantum mechanics and whatnot still sounds to me like a bunch of mythological mumbo jumbo, but . . . okay, you have the cat in the box. In one world the cat is alive and in other word the cat is dead. But what's between those worlds?" More workers turn to watch us.

"Somewhere else," I say, hearing Wendell once again. *All energy has to come from somewhere.*

"I suppose that's as good a name as any other."

"But wouldn't that resource eventually end, like oil reserves?"

"We don't know," she says, throwing her hands out. "And we won't until we try. The fact that you're able to create and destroy energy itself suggests that energy is not a finite nor reciprocal resource. Thus, everything we thought we knew about energy is incorrect. Might be true in our world but it isn't in . . . others. Whatever source feeds energy into your brain could be harnessed to power the entire planet. Everything from electric cars to entire cities on clean power grids." She beams. There's a giddiness to her voice. "This engine could be miniaturized into artificial hearts that never stop working. It means aircraft that easily break the atmosphere, oxygen generators on the moon, terraforming other planets."

She continues speaking as we navigate through the remaining construction. I stop listening. There's some kind of portal in my brain. That's . . . well, in a world of seven billion people odds are something like this will happen somewhere. Even if the odds against it are infinite.

" . . . Those are a long time away, but the first step toward them is here," she says.

Is that where Wendell is? Another world? A gap between worlds?

"The applications are limitless. And they're all because of you." She stops. All that's left in front of us is the freight transport and the ride back to the laboratory where every day my brain is opened and recorded while I'm pushed, tweaked, and prodded into giving the desired result. When they don't get that . . .

I'm a lab rat running the same maze over and over.

"Isn't that worth a little frustration?" she says with her brows up and a puffy-cheeked smile.

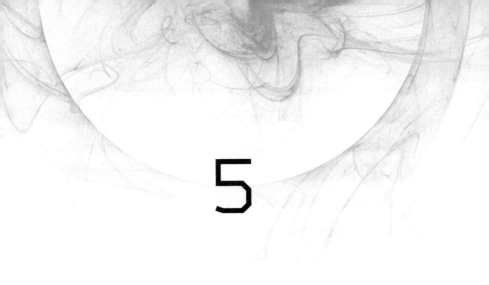

5

"**H**OW DO YOU FEEL NOW?" BURNETT ASKS AS WE reenter the test lab through the observation side door. "Better? More motivated?"

"Yeah," I say, because that's what I know she wants me to say. Solar Flare, the complex, multiple worlds, the space between those worlds, there's still so much to think about before I know how to react. I'm not even sure I can trust her after everything she's done.

"Good," she says.

I follow her across the gridded floor toward the door the on the other side, the subject side, the door through which I usually pass. Rogers and

McPherson are waiting on the outside, as always. It may be too early for lunch.

"Well, no session this afternoon," she says, reaching for the touch screen next to the subject side door. Typically Winger opens the door for me, but without him, Burnett had to walk me all the way back. "Hope you enjoy your day off," the door begins to open, "because tomorrow—" Delgado stands on the other side.

His eyes dart between the two of us. "Doctor," he says, "we'll take the subject from here."

Every hint of cheerfulness drains from her face. She stares down at the block of pins attached to the chest of his uniform. "Yes, sir," she says.

Delgado's personal guard forms a path leading from the door to him. He motions for me to step forward. I do so. The door slides closed behind me.

No Rogers or McPherson. Delgado and his unknown soldiers. They aren't the twelve who accompanied me the first day. They may not even be the same as those who were present during my last conversation with the general. Their masks make it impossible to tell.

Delgado places his hands behind his back as I approach. "I hope you enjoyed your little tour," he says. He turns and steps away. "Come," he says over his shoulder, "You don't need to worry about retribution. Every one of the men around you have made more terrorizing threats against me."

"I'm sure they have," I say, stepping behind him.

The guards remain in two columns behind us as we approach the elevator. He presses his fingertips to the elevator screen. "I expect you now have a greater understanding of our mission here." The door opens immediately. He gestures for me to enter first, then him, then the guards fill in around us. The door closes. He stares straight ahead.

"To be honest, I have no interest in theories and science and whatever idealist bunk the doctor fed you. All that concerns me is results. If the result of this project is an engine that weakens the global influence of our enemies and leads to fewer of our serving men and women dying for oil, then it will have been worth every dollar."

The elevator door opens. I know I'm to step out first.

"What I'm not sure of," he says, stepping behind me with the guards back around us, "is you."

"Funny," I say, "I feel the same way."

"Until recently I'd been quite pleased with your progress. You'd been showing yourself to be a reliable asset. But then . . . " We walk past the intersections for the showers and medical room. "An unreliable asset is no asset. It is nothing." McPherson and Rogers come into view as we enter the waiting area between my room, the mess, and the detention center. This portion of the complex feels tiny compared to everything else I've seen today. Delgado turns to face me for a moment before stepping away. He opens the living quarters door.

"You are an asset or you are nothing. We will see soon."

"Where are you?"

Everywhere. Nowhere. Take your pick.

I sit on the bed and stare at the floor in my room. The room belongs to someone else but it's mine in the sense that I use it and live in it. Meanwhile, Wendell lives in and uses my head, yet it's still my head. At least I always thought that. The idea was there but I'd never really considered that Wendell, the voice from when I was a little boy, may actually exist somewhere else at the same time as he's contained in my mind. It may be that my head isn't *my* head at all. I walk from the side of the bed to the wall near the desk and back. My bed. My desk.

"Can you see this?" I wave my hands alternating in front of my face.

Flailing arms. Yes.

"And you can obviously hear me."

Obviously.

"What else? Can you feel? When I'm hurt do you feel that pain?"

No.

"Frustration? Anger? Annoyance?"

I feel all of that. But not yours. I have plenty of my own.

I'd read all about the multiverse idea before, that in the expanse of the universe are an infinite number of alternate realities covering every possible world. Small changes: Worlds where Sarsgaard didn't act like a jerk to Dr. Burnett, or where David didn't cut my eye during the fight. Big changes: Worlds where I was never brought to this place or one where my parents are . . . still around. Bigger changes: Worlds where World War II never happened or ended differently, worlds where I don't exist. And totally bizarre changes: Worlds populated by sentient cinnamon buns or where our number system is based on nine because that's how many fingers we have. The possibilities, the infinite possibilities, are literally too much to even consider.

I guess on an intellectual level it makes some kind of sense, given how little we know of the entire universe, having hardly traveled beyond our own tiny planet—for me, having hardly lived outside of my own head—but to have possible confirmation of that theory is . . . staggering. And to have it because of me. That feels kinda badass.

But then it doesn't.

If my brain contains a window into another world, what does that mean for me? If everything I can do, the lifting, turning, throwing, stopping objects in midflight, even seeing into other people's memories or my own, is because of access to some extra-dimensional energy, then why do I have this other being in my mind? Is Wendell a cause or an effect?

"Where are you?" I say again, even though I'm sure he won't answer.

I am everywhere that you are.

This is making my head hurt.

I take a different tack. "So, if you can see and hear everything in the same way that I do, does that mean you can move like I do?"

I am an observer.

"Like me when I see into the past. Can you do that?"

Yes. It is the same thing except that I am not limited to your world alone, as you are. I see them all.

It's possible that Wendell isn't actually a person at all, at least not the way that we'd usually think of a person. Maybe he is the energy. No. Because when he isn't here, isn't looking in or whatever it is he does, I still have the same abilities. They may not be as sharp or accessible, but I can still use them. He can't be the cause. He could be an effect.

"So it's true?" I say. "Parallel worlds?"

In a sense.

"You've known this the whole time and never thought to tell me?"

No others are important.

I chuckle pathetically. "Why don't you just answer the fucking question? Where are you? How is it I can do these things? What, in general, is going on?"

Because none of that will help you now. They are distractions.

"You're a distraction."

No, I am your purpose. The doctor, the general, they are distractions. Have you not noticed that every time you come close to defying their commands, one of them appears with a reason not to? At the school. This room. That machine. They only give you information when they think you need to be controlled.

"It's to stop me from doing something that could get me killed."

No. It is to stop them from doing something that could get them killed.

"I wouldn't do that."

I know, Odin. You would not.

I turn from the bed to the wall yet again. Suddenly this room we share feels infinitely small.

They are right about one thing, the laws of this reality do not apply to you. You are above all rules. Natural and unnatural.

"I guess you weren't watching yesterday."

You have not tried. Your method was fine when it was books and furniture, trivial tricks and prestidigitation. It is time to move beyond that. Stop focusing on why and start focusing on why not.

"You sound like those motivational speakers on Sunday morning infomercials."

Except that for you it is true.

I close my eyes. *Does he see nothing but black too? When I sleep does he sleep?*

"How do you know?"

I have seen it happen. I have seen what this power can do. I have done it myself.

"How?"

I have used it where I am.

"Between worlds?"

Between everywhere and nowhere.

I place my palm flat to the wall. A solid barrier. "What is it? What's it like?"

It is everything that was and is. It makes everything that can be.

"Makes?"

Where you are has presence and laws. Where I am has only possibility. I can shape things as I wish, but I know that none of it is real.

I push off the wall to resume pacing. "But why am I the only one you can talk to?"

Is it not obvious?

He once referred to "us."

My first day in Ben and Aida's house, the only time I ever saw Wendell outside of my mind, he was there. He was small and unclear, but he looked like me. Same eyes, hair, skin, same nose and face. I assumed that it was a function of my wanting someone to relate to. I'd envisioned a friend like me.

"Us," I say, remembering the vision I had in the bowling alley. Rippling energy. Floating above the road. Vehicles pushing back. "This is us."

Exactly.

"You're another me. Me from another reality."

No. I am you from this reality.

"How—"

I have seen this life before.

I feel a jolt through every part of my body, a shake like I'd stuck a fork into an electrical outlet. It's painful and paralyzing yet somehow, almost pleasant.

That is why I first came to you, that day in that house. I wanted to help you, guide you to the life you were born for. Turn you toward a world where you belong.

"Where I belong?"

You were never meant to be here. You are an anomaly. That is why you can do the things you can do. Because you do not belong here. You are an orphan.

There's a warmth in the center of my head.

I lost my chance in this world. I failed it. That is why I have come to help you.

"What the hell does that mean, lost my chance?"

I displaced myself in the universe. I thought I could return but found you instead. There was nothing I could do. I decided to help you do what I could not.

I stop halfway to the bed. *My* bed. "To control me you mean. Just like them."

I choose exile over failure. You are my redemption, Odin. You are my chance to make things right.

"I am not your second chance. I'm no one's puppet.

You are, Odin. One way or another you will become a tool. The only question is, who will you belong to?

6

IT'S NICE TO BREAK SOMETHING.

Jagged chunks roll from the table to the floor. The air around the target is thick enough with cement dust that Hawthorne has to wipe his goggles clean before stepping in to replace the slab on the table. He holds his breath while bending to hoist the concrete into position. I swing the five-pound ball around as easily as my arm. I don't even need to picture the motion. I do it. As soon as Hawthorne is set in his position several feet away from the target area, I destroy the fresh slab with a flick of my finger. Strike, headshot, whatever. They mean the same thing: broken.

I do not belong here. That's what Wendell said. This is not my world, this world where everything I've ever done has been controlled and contained. Wendell and his redemption. Delgado and his asset. Burnett and her machine. What do I have that's truly mine? I don't even have my own life. Haven't for years. I'm a ghost, a shadow, an anomaly, an orphan—the words Wendell used—in every way.

I don't see the ball fly anymore. I hear the explosion, see the pieces fall, swing the ball around and wait for a new slab to break. Who cares about the forces involved? Perry has long since given up on tracking the speed of every throw.

Wendell could be lying. Another of his manipulations. Burnett as well with her well-meaning science. The same science that she used to keep me docile for years. The day after I threatened Delgado, the authority of this place, suddenly here's this amazing machine that will save the world. Isn't it so wonderful? Sure, but this is the same project that told me if I didn't bring attention to myself, they'd leave me alone. The same project that told me I was responsible for my parents' deaths after spending years conditioning me not to think about them. Why should I trust them—trust her—now, after everything they've done? For all I know, Solar Flare could be a weapon.

Then, right after her big reveal, here's Delgado. His sharp stare and melodic tone reminding me of what happens if I disobey. Back into the cells. Or worse. Carrot and stick.

I could search through every interaction they've ever had. I would find nothing. They know better than to speak with each other. Even Winger sends his research to someone else so I can't view it myself. As for Wendell, he's the one person I can never read. Ironic that the only person who's a true mystery is the one living in my mind.

Another slab bursts into chunks and dust. I treat the metal ball like a muscle. The brain tells it what to do and the muscle reacts. I don't need to think about how or why the movement happens. Like life itself, it just happens.

Wendell told me when I was a kid that in all the worlds in the universe, this is the only one where I was born. Does that mean that every other version of myself is him? He says he can't see the future, yet he claims that he's lived this life before. He says he exiled himself, but that this is still his world. No. This is my world. My life. I will make it what I want it to be. Not him. Not Burnett. Not Delgado. No one decides what happens to me except me.

Another slab disappears into bits and dust. Hawthorne waves away the dust cloud building around the table. He pushes the rubble away as he steps forward. Perry stares from her position near the monitor room window. Her eyes behind the goggles look like they're about to pop out from her skull. I wonder if I could make them do that. If I really wanted to.

"More," I say to Hawthorne as he flees from the lab table. He glances over to Winger behind the glass. Winger gives an emphatic thumbs up. Delgado maintains his typical spot in the back of the room near the door. His arms are folded over his chest. His chin is up and pointed at me. I probably couldn't have broken the bulletproof glass in front of them before. I bet I could now. Hawthorne places a second inch-thick block on the table in front of the first. I swing the metal ball, my fist, into position.

They said this whole experiment is because of me. What they don't say is that I'm the experiment. They made me. They created my reality, my family, my life, my thoughts, my actions. They crafted my upbringing in such a way that the only options I'd consider are those they anticipated. Whether or not I originated in this world, it has made me an inextricable part of it. A piece of metal fashioned into a key to open precisely one door among millions.

The front slab shatters. The second one does not. It's dented and cracked, but it's still intact. I pull the ball back a few feet and fire it once more. The slab is already damaged. It doesn't take much to break it.

"Again," I bark at Hawthorne. "Like that."

I remember Kevin. All I knew at the time was how much I hated him and everything he'd said and done since the first day of high school. How scared I was of being beaten again in front of everyone. In front of Evelyn. I wanted him to pay for what he'd done to me, to my friends, for what he said about her. I didn't think about it.

Then there was the rest of them, Eric, Dylan, Ross, T.J., David the traitor. They could have actually killed me. It was a survival instinct to make them stop. It was self-defense. At least stopping David's fist was. After that it became a lesson. I wanted them to suffer. I wanted them to feel a pain in their bones every time the weather turned cold so they would remember what happened to them. I wanted them to come back to school with casts and bruises for everyone to see. I wanted Brent to drop to his knees begging me to spare him. "I didn't mean it," he'd say, "they threatened me, they made me." I'd forgive him. I would. But inside he'd always know. They'd all know. I am not their toy. Do not play with me.

I growl as I thrust one hand forward. Both blocks become one as they break from the inside out. That's the way breaking happens. From the inside out.

Hawthorne approaches the six remaining blocks on the pile by the table. I can hear him preparing to heft up another pair.

"Stop," I say. Every eye is on me. I know they are. Delgado tilts his head in curiosity. He now has a holstered pistol strapped to his waist. I see myself in the middle of the room a second ago. The electrodes from my head anchor me to the panel in the floor, like a cyborg from the movies. An alien for study. I am, after all, from another world.

I move one hand to lift a block from the pile and onto the table. I place a second behind it. Is this what they expected when they made me? Are they satisfied with their experiment? Their creation, their bubble baby, sheltered and conditioned. Am I what Dr. Burnett made me to be? Her machine?

Am I Delgado's asset now? Or am I Wendell's second chance?

Two blocks on the table. Two piles on the floor. That table top is getting cluttered. I brush the pieces of concrete off like the wind. Leave the debris on the floor for them. They created this mess, they can clean it.

It's warm, like sitting in a park on a sunny day. I can feel it starting in the middle of my skull and emanating outward from the top of my head to the tips of my fingers to the pads of my feet. It's the same feeling as the jolt when Wendell laughs, only this time it feels as though it's something internal, starting from inside, and not something external being forced through. I'm not holding a fork in an outlet. I am the outlet.

Three blocks. Focus. Five pounds of metal and three inches of concrete. One inch takes one thousand nine hundred newtons to break. I turn to look at Delgado through the glass. I lock onto the sharp points at the center of his pupils. He stares back. Would the amount of force be multiplied by three or to the power of three?

No matter. Three at once. Straight through the center.

This is what I needed the whole time. Turn logic off. Make it happen. Stop asking why, start asking why not. Why strain to stay hidden within their rules? Why not enjoy this?

One block left intact on the ground. Too easy. I let the ball drop to the floor with a thud so they remember how solid it is. I lift the slab in the air. I bring it halfway between me and the pile of shattered rocks strew across the laboratory floor. Big finish. I look at Winger, his expression contoured into equal parts fear and excitement, and onto Delgado. The flexed muscles in his jaw are outcrops on the cliffside. I clench my fist. The concrete grinds to dust. In the end, everything becomes dust.

Winger's mouth drops, a big gap in his hairy face. His focus spins madly from Delgado to Perry to Hawthorne, looking for someone to celebrate with. The two in the room with me are stunned in place, like test dummies strapped to poles when the collision comes. Winger throws his hands up as though he'd actually accomplished something. I can hear Winger's exuberance even out here, through the glass. I don't have to look.

Winger slams his hand onto the speaker button. "That was amazing! No idea what Dr. Burnett told you yesterday but I wish she'd said it sooner. These patterns, they're—" He looks around at the others again. Perry and Hawthorne almost tremble, and Delgado turns his jutted jaw toward Winger. "I don't even know how to describe it." He looks from me to Hawthorne in the corner, the rubble not far from his feet. "You guys okay in there?"

"I think so," says Hawthorne, brushing the dust off his clothing.

"Uhhh," says Winger, as though he's completely forgotten he was pressing the speaker button, "Odin, you can go get some lunch or, hell, do whatever you want."

I remove the electrodes from my head. Delgado turns to leave.

"We'll try to get this data analyzed before the afternoon session."

"Next time," I say, dropping the last of the wires to the floor, "make it a challenge."

McPherson and Rogers tend to relax a bit outside while I'm in the lab. They talk about what they think I'm doing, how cool it must be to levitate forks and throw basketballs with my mind, theories they've heard from other soldiers around the base on what's contained within this underground complex—

"It's a weapon, isn't it? Some kind of top secret electromagnetic bomb to disable all enemy communications."

"No, it's an alien, like in Area 51."

"I heard it's the frozen head of John F. Kennedy and they're working on reviving him."

—And how difficult it is to not correct their blithering nonsense.

They stiffen as the lab door slides open, fingers over their triggers, safeties off. I step into the empty room and straight for the elevator, ignoring the door which bypasses the lab toward the fabrication area, where Burnett led me yesterday.

"What was it this time?" McPherson asks, catching up. He reminds me of Andre when I'd receive a letter in the mail.

"It was something to see," I say without pausing, except to let one of them press their fingers to the screen that summons the elevator. I can't even press a button in this place by myself.

We ride the elevator up together, the two of them flanking me with body armor and automatic weapons, M4A1s, the fully automatic version of the M4 Carbines that both McPherson and Rogers used in Iraq and Afghanistan—standard for Army Rangers, Army Special Forces, Navy SEALs and other special operations use. I qualify for that.

Firing rate of seven hundred to nine hundred rounds per minute. Box magazines loaded with two extra clips in pouches on their belts. Upper handles replaced with red-dot laser sites. Standard M9 sidearm strapped to their right legs. Fifteen-round magazine with one in the chamber. I wonder if I could pop open the strap over the handle of their pistols, and if they'd notice.

"So," says McPherson, staring at the closed door in front of us, "can you tell us the experiment, or are you sworn to secrecy?"

I bet, if I really tried, I could pry these doors open. Lift or drop this elevator wherever I wanted it to go. To the top, the aboveground portion with the wide walkways and the bars over every opening. Pry the doors and walk outside where the walls and towers surround us. It'd be nice to see the sun again. Or even clouds. A damp shower is no substitute for the smell of rain.

How long has it been? Weeks? Months? Couldn't have been that long. Days don't matter when every one of them is the same. Go here at this time, do this, lunch, back to the lab, dinner, lights out. The only thing that changes are the meals and the men who watch while I eat them. At least with school, the classes were at different times. There was summer to look forward to. There would be an end.

Mom's calendar says June 28th, her friend Trish's birthday. Maybe I'll get a day off on the Fourth of July, being in a military facility and all. Not much point in seeing what else is happening. Mom, Dad, Andre, none of them matter down here. It'll only make me miss them.

I always liked the start of the summer, before boredom begins and the days become too long and too hot. Vacation eventually blurs in the way school does. Early summer is novel. It feels like there are a million possibilities and enough time to do everything. I'd probably be preparing for senior year, listening to Brent and them talk about all the freedom we're gonna have once school is over. They'd pressure me to make a move on Evelyn, ask her to prom, something before we go our separate ways. Last chance to do her before she goes to college, Richard would probably say, where she can do anyone she wants. We all can. Yeah, David, the traitor, would say. I can't wait to be free.

The Project would never allow me up there, outside, even within the complex walls, not while they can still use me. No way they'd let me stroll into the daylight, give me a lift back to town to say "Bye" to my classmates, the few who may remain, before they begin whatever is next for them. I'd tell Andre not to wonder about me, where I've gone, what I'm doing, and, above all else, not to follow me. "Don't worry," I'd say, "Mom and Dad will always take care of you. Better than they took care of me. Because you are theirs." None of this will happen. Even when they—*they*—don't need me anymore.

The elevator doors open. We, me ahead with Rogers and McPherson behind, step into the same recycled air we've breathed hundreds of times before. We step through the carefully maintained passages with unstained white walls that are cleaned every night. Each sign, camera, fire extinguisher, and light is specifically placed within its own cubby hole made to fit that individual item, a little apartment, like mine, to keep it separate from everything else. Safe from the monster that roams these halls, a monster that requires two armed guards and a regular schedule at all times.

There's no one in the cafeteria today. Maybe they're clamoring for a piece of that amazing data Winger got from our session. Maybe they're stuck in their own containers. Makes no difference to me.

"Not today," I say. "I'm going to my room."

"It's lunch time," Rogers says.

"I don't care." I turn to walk away from the mess. He steps into my path. The bottom of his chin is points at me.

"You are scheduled for lunch and nothing else."

I lift my eyes and nothing else to him. He places his finger over the trigger of his weapon. Behind me, a second ago, McPherson motioned to Rogers to keep the weapon down. I could spin Rogers's head backward before he has time to think about firing.

Actually no, I couldn't. Rogers has parents who sent him a care package every month while he was deployed regardless of where he was. He has a younger sister who's getting married in September. He's promised to serve as a groomsman. I'm not like him or McPherson, or Carter, Harris, Delgado, any of the others. I can't separate a soldier from their humanity. I can imagine it as a possibility, and have the ability to do it, but I can't follow through. They are not tools to me.

"You sure you don't want food?" McPherson says, his voice soft as cotton. "Now's the only time until dinner."

I stare at Rogers. Bags hang under his brown eyes like a hound dog. He's always had them, even when he was my age. He tried sleeping more, using moisturizers, nothing worked. He tried lying down with sliced cucumbers over his eyes, like in spa magazine ads and commercials, as the epitome of rest and rejuvenation. He didn't like having wet things over his eyes and the smell became repulsive. He steps back. I walk on.

Empty halls, blank walls, nothing. We pass no one. Another fingerprint scanner to enter the door to my living quarters. The common area isn't common if only eight people are permitted to enter it. I continue to the door to my apartment. The only door absolutely anyone can open, if the guards outside allow it. I guess passive security isn't enough for me. Mine has to be living.

The moment I close the door behind me he speaks, exactly as I thought he would.

Impressive. Truly impressive.

"Leave me alone."

You are finally moving beyond limits.

"You heard me, right? I said leave me alone. Go watch someone else."

He waits long enough to make me think that maybe he's gone.

Another time.

I feel him leave. It's the first moment alone I've had all day.

A buzzer has replaced the single knock in telling me when it's time to leave my room.

Outside, Harris has replaced Rogers and Carter has replaced McPherson. Other than the faces, and the fact that Harris is about five inches taller than Rogers while Carter is two inches shorter than McPherson, everything is exactly the same: the armor, the guns, the pausing for doors, the slightly offset formation of them to the side and just far enough back that I can't reach them without making an effort. We are an exact copy of this morning, and yesterday, and the day before.

There's a noise as we step through the door out of my living area. A low murmur, a rumble of activity. I see three soldiers in the passage of the mess hall as we go by. Another two on their way to the medical center. Two more at the elevator.

Delgado ordered additional security immediately after the session this morning. In case of "another situation" he said. He probably means the thing with the glass two days ago. I thought he'd been more terrorized by his own men. At least today won't blend in with every other day.

Here's the short march to the lab door. Carter and Harris stand at the ready, waiting for me to enter so they can relax, put the safeties on their guns, and talk about what it's like guarding the virus that could cause a worldwide zombie outbreak. The lab door slides open. I enter. There are Winger and Delgado behind the glass.

I hope they give me something to break.

7

"**T**HEY'RE SAYING IT'S BECAUSE THE MACHINE IS nearly complete and they don't want any possible saboteurs."

Burnett looks around at the armored soldiers who just happen to be passing by while we're here having dinner. Nine soldiers, including Harris and Carter, four currently in motion through the room. Others will coincidentally enter immediately after they leave.

We normally have our meetings in the common room, but not anymore. Not since she toured me through the back area of the facility. Not since I witnessed the construction of Solar Flare. But mostly, not since I learned to not be limited by physical laws. Harris and Carter turned her away at the door this evening while I was watching an old *Simpsons* episode. She was told that I was no longer allowed any visitors outside of public places. She came here and waited for me to arrive.

She continues, "There have been a lot of leaks lately. Not about this project, but plenty of others. Delgado and his superiors at the Pentagon, they claim that's what this protection is for. To make sure there are no internal problems."

Guards are posted at almost every corner now. They're in constant motion through the halls as I'm escorted from my room to the elevator, to the lab, to the mess, and from any starting point to any destination. No extras have been added to my detail and not a single soldier has entered the testing lab. That's how they're trying to show that this added "protection" is for anything other than me. That's also how I know it's entirely because of me. What I don't yet know is how pointing their presence out benefits Burnett.

Burnett leans back to one side of her chair. She

rests on one arm while stretching the other. It's her power pose. The position she uses when she's trying to control me.

"Has it been a bother at all?"

"Barely noticed," I say.

Her look tells me she knows exactly what I mean. "Any thought on what I told you the last time we spoke?" She wants to know if I've mentioned to Wendell the theory she outlined in the hangar where Solar Flare is being constructed, if Wendell can confirm or deny that theory. But she isn't asking to know if the theory she presented is true. She's asking to see if she retains enough influence over me that I'd relay her idea to my . . . friend.

"That theory seems accurate," I say.

"Has it been confirmed?"

"I believe so." This is true. It also doesn't reveal that I've figured her out.

She nods, one cheek puffed in a reassured smile. She looks around the room, as though she'd some-how now be able to see the threads which could divide our reality from another, the divisions which separate them, and the decisions which cause our divergence.

"I don't belong here," I say.

She breathes in deeply.

"I understand why you would feel that way," she says, "but trust me, this is the safest place you could possibly be right now. There's nothing that happens here without a reason or a plan."

I'm sure it doesn't. "No," I say, looking her dead in the eyes, "I don't belong here."

She tilts her head, then her eyebrows rise without her speaking. I bite my tongue to prevent myself from saying what I'd like. *I'm only here because of you and your conditioning. Because of everything you did to mess with my mind so much, I can't tell which parts are naturally me and which are influentially you.*

"What do you mean?"

I've said too much already. I need to lead her to a different line of thinking.

"He's seen this all before," I say. "My friend."

She leans forward and brings one hand in front of her mouth.

"He says that I'm an anomaly." I glance at the pair of soldiers approaching on their totally normal patrol of the facility. "That's why I can do the things I can do."

"Are you sure that's the reason?"

I can't be sure of anything. I haven't been since you, Doctor, took over my life.

"An anomaly?" she says.

"An orphan."

"But that's it exactly, isn't it?" she says, perking up. "Anyone else would be ordinary. Just another regular person, no more special than your average no one, in the sense that we are, of course, all special little snowflakes, but snowflakes nonetheless. It's the rock or the leaf that stands out." She smiles. "Whether or not you belonged here at first, you do now. It's because of you that any of this," she spins her finger to indicate this conversation, this complex, "is possible. Another person wouldn't have been anywhere near as useful."

She's doing it again. Exactly as I thought she would.

Anytime I come close to losing purpose or defying their rules, one of them shows up. That's been her job from the start, keep me in their program. From the moment I walked into Ben and Aida's house, through the mornings we had in her office, every moment I spent at home with my parents—who were following her instructions in how to mold me into their desired form—and up to this very moment, her task has been to keep me on track. Now, with soldiers patrolling through like prison guards after a riot, she's here to reassure me that everything is fine: Don't get discouraged. I understand how you feel. You're special. You can't dwell on the past. Forget that your whole life was manufactured. Forget the world outside these walls. Forget that you're being held captive in an underground facility and forced to undergo testing every goddamn day. Forgot all of that. Remember only that you are helping to us to build this machine. It's amazing. It's going to save the world. And it's because of you.

Forget that she was behind it all.

———⌣———

There was a meeting in a conference room two weeks after my parents died. This was before even Delgado, Braxton, or Choi got involved with the project, but there were a dozen of them, Burnett included. A man in thick glasses presented them with packets of newspaper clippings on the accident. Little paragraphs described a couple falling into the street and being hit by an oncoming truck while their five-year-old son stood on the curb watching. He showed them the local news coverage of some blonde lady in a red suit with a microphone standing in front of the street that police had closed to everyone except residents while they investigated what had happened. I'd already been taken to the station. I don't remember much of the incident. I don't want to look now. Better to follow this.

Another man wondered why this story was important. People die in traffic every day, it's like reporting a heart attack or a shooting. What's the point?

The man in the glasses replied that this one is different. The truck driver swore the couple was nowhere near the curb as he drove ahead. Said the woman was walking the other way. Other witnesses reported the same thing, they say that . . . No . . . Focus on Burnett . . . She's the important part.

"It's a risk," she said, looking around at the old guys in starched shirts staring at her from around the table. "He'll be fragile; anyone would be after something like this, especially at that age."

"What would you suggest?" asked a man with thick, black hair and heavy jowls.

"A new environment," she said, "one where he can be contained and watched, guided as much as possible. We can't risk him going to another family that may not understand his situation. We definitely can't trust putting him into the state system. The last thing we need is another at-risk youth, especially one who can potentially manipulate the world around him. It would be tragic."

She paused a moment, allowing them to imagine the consequences.

"We need to keep him in a place where we can follow his progress at all times, even in the home. Instill in him the values and the virtues that we need so if he develops the way we hope, he'll be willing to help without having to force him."

"Are you suggesting we keep him under twenty-four-hour watch?" asked a man with a square face and squinted eyes.

"I'm suggesting we have our own people take care of him. Most of our character is learned in childhood, primarily from what we see our parents do. We need to know that this child is raised with traits and habits optimal for our purpose. We need to engineer him."

"Won't he figure this out?" said heavy face.

"If we do this correctly, then that won't matter. He'll understand. He may even appreciate it."

"What about his parents?" asked squinty eyes. "Won't he be curious about them?"

"Not if we teach him not to be. He'll need guidance, especially after such a traumatic event. A loss, a new place, a new family, it wouldn't be unreasonable for a child in such a situation to require the help of a counselor. It also offers us a chance to further reinforce the lessons we want him to learn. Repetition. That's how we guide him to make the choices we want on his own. Nothing else would work."

"Very well," says the man in the very back of the room, dark skinned with a shaved head. "Burns will help you filter possible candidates and you can oversee the operation yourself."

"Oversee, sir?"

"Be the boy's therapist. Help reinforce the values we want him to have. All that other stuff you said. Can you handle this?"

"I . . . I believe so."

"We'll need more than belief if this is going to work."

"Yes, sir. It will be done, sir."

"Good. Put together your proposal and send it to me by noon tomorrow." He looks at the others. "Are we finished?"

"Yes, sir," says the man who distributed the packages.

"Okay," says the man at the end. He stands to button his suit jacket. I've never seen him before. "Burnett, start talking with Burns immediately about any personnel we have available to raise this boy." Burnett glances at the man with the jowls. "Begin with people who are already familiar with the project and work out from there. Better to use one of our own than to bring in someone new."

He pauses then, looking from Dr. Burnett to every one of the faces staring up at him.

"Hah. Burnett and Burns. Sounds like a sitcom."

She's the only one who doesn't laugh.

"—Not bothered?" she says.

She leans back in the chair, only her eyes following another set of soldiers approaching from behind me.

"What was that?"

"I asked if you sure you're not bothered. By the extra protection."

"Maybe a little bit." Better she think that's the case than something else. I try to remain as still as possible so no one will notice anything strange. Not her, and not the soldiers.

"I saw the recordings from the other day. Quite a show."

"Thanks."

"What did it feel like doing that? Doing things that are theoretically more impossible than anything else you've done . . . if anything can technically be 'more impossible'?"

I shake my head. "It didn't feel like anything. It just happened."

"I'd think it would be exciting."

I shrug. She tilts her head at this. Perhaps I'm being a bit too casual. "Maybe motivation makes things easier," I say. "Having a sense of purpose." Don't lay it on too thick. "You know what I mean?"

She nods. "I hoped it would." She doesn't completely believe me. "It was quite spectacular. The footage, I mean. Mindblowing, so to speak. You're comfortable with these kinds of tests?"

"I'm fine."

"Are you sure?" she says, trying to make me feel as though I'm giving my approval to continue.

"Yes."

"Well, carry on then. I'm sure the results will be amazing." Reinforce. She has spent this entire conversation trying to say one thing: Stay under their control. For me, she has been saying something different: Don't believe anything.

8

MY PARENTS TOLD ME I WAS THERE TO PLAY A FEW games, talk, ask questions, even draw pictures, if that's what I wanted. Only no television, no video games, no toys, nothing could enter the room except me and my feelings.

The office door opened. "Hello, Odin," the lady in the dark blue skirt and jacket said in a soft voice, "I'm Dr. Burnett."

My parents had to push me forward. Then I saw the view: an entire wall of glass showing miles of roads and buildings. The sun reflected off hundreds of windows like waves in the water I vaguely remembered flying over on the airplane when I arrived in my new home, mountains and trees in the distance, tiny people moving slowly past each other as ants do following a single path. I felt like I could see more of the world in that second than I ever had before, even from the plane. I stood back to take it all in.

"It's cool, isn't it?" Dr. Burnett said from behind me. I didn't even hear the door close.

I nodded. She was shorter than my teachers or parents, all four of them, but somehow I felt smaller with her. A mouse staring up at a lion.

"You can walk right up to it. It's very safe."

I did. Looking over the side was like flying. I towered over people who had towered over me. I moved my hands in front of my face to cover them with my fingers. So small. Even the buildings, some extending above my head, most ending below in dirty roofs with plants brown and withered from neglect. There were the cars, like toys, bunched together behind white lines waiting for their chance to go. They zoomed by so close to the pedestrians. Then I felt nervous, partly because of the height, the thin glass which separated me from gravity, and partly because at any second one of those people could trip and fall into the street. I knew that far too well. I jumped backward, shaking.

"It's completely safe," Burnett said, knocking her fist on the glass, "I promise."

The leather couch was nothing but cushions. There was a small table in the middle and a chair that matched the couch. An asymmetrical collection of finger paintings occupied the back of the door. Bookshelves along two walls rivaled the library from my old school, the one we'd go to once a week and sit on the floor near the front door while the librarian, Mr. Douglas, would read us a book he'd chosen, usually one with a lot of rhyming in it. The books in Burnett's office were darker colored and thicker than my arm. Between the couch and the window wall was another shelf, half as tall and loaded with games and puzzles. She had checkers, chess, playing cards, board games I'd never heard of, colorful boxes with friendly letters written on every side, and even different metal shapes with rings attached.

"Would you like to play a game, Odin?"

I looked up at her and said nothing. Behind her was the desk, a big wooden box on legs with a fancy lamp, a pen sticking out of a stand, and a very thin computer monitor. The desk sat in the back corner, parallel to the window, as though teetering on a cliff.

"Let's play a game," she said. She knelt down next to me. I stepped away from her. "What would you like?"

I shrugged.

She flipped through the different boxes with their bright pictures of smiling, cartoon people on the front. "How about this one?" she said, holding a purple box with a fancy design and weird writing that looked like squares and slashes. "Do you know this game?"

I shook my head.

"That's okay, I'll teach you." She placed the box down on the coffee table and sat in the big pillow chair facing the even bigger pillow couch. "You can sit down if you want."

I had to plant my hands to jump up onto the seat. I sank down, as though the couch cushion would swallow me whole.

She placed the box under the table between us. The board was a piece of wood with a multi-colored star with six sides and a bunch of little holes carved into it at regular spaces. "Do you have a favorite color, Odin?"

I nodded.

"What color is that?"

I point at the green end of the star.

"Okay, you can be green."

We played for almost fifty minutes, Burnett explaining the game to me as we went.

Afterwards I was told to sit outside while my parents went in. The couches out there weren't as big or soft as the one inside, but the table in front of them had more of the metal shapes on it. I hopped on the center cushion and grabbed a small pair of horseshoes attached by a chain with a ring between them.

"Are you sure it's him?" Mom asked inside Burnett's office. "He hasn't done anything unusual. In fact he's hardly even said anything."

My parents sat much farther onto the couch than I did.

"They're sure it's him," said Dad.

"This is a difficult adjustment," Burnett replied, "He needs time to feel comfortable."

"How long is that supposed to take?"

She shook her head. "Every child is different and he's been through a lot."

"But how do we know he's safe to have around the house?" Mom's tone was quick and elevated. She leaned forward without resting on her hands or elbows. "We have a child of our own to take care of."

"Two children of our own," Dad said calmly, elbows on his legs and hands folded. "He's ours now, too."

"He's theirs, we're just holding him for the—"

"There's no way to tell how long it'll take to adjust," Burnett said. Mom looked annoyed at being cut off. "But whatever you do, please treat him like you do your other son. No adoption works if the children are treated differently, and the last thing we want is for him to grow up thinking he's second class to anyone. We need him to see everyone as equally capable and qualified. That way, he'll be willing to use his abilities to help others rather than either hurting them or helping himself. We need you to reinforce a feeling of altruism."

Mom crossed her arms in front of her.

"Have you enrolled him in school yet?"

"He started last week," Dad said. "He doesn't speak there either, but that's probably normal for anyone starting halfway through the year."

"And how is he with your other son?"

"Fine. Andre probably doesn't even know he's there."

"Not at that age."

"I thought I heard Odin trying to talk to him once, but he was in his room by himself, talking like there was another boy with him." Burnett nodded. "Is that strange?"

"No," she said, "a lot of kids do that at his age. I'll bring it up to him. I think after another couple of sessions, he'll be comfortable enough to start engagement. We'll begin then, moving him away from thinking about his parents and seeing what exactly he can do."

She glanced over to Mom, whose arms were still folded and her jaw tight.

"It may not feel like it now, but this is all progress. What we do today will have a profound effect on what happens years from now." Burnett sat back to look at them both. "It's important to always remember that."

I was bored by the time they came back outside.

"All right, Odin," Burnett said, Dad and Mom behind her, "I'll see you next we—" She looked down at the table, five metal rings next to five different metal shapes. "You did all of those?"

I looked up at Dad, then Mom, then down to the couch beneath me.

"That's amazing, Odin," Burnett said. "You're a very smart boy."

It was immediately after that, as Mom, Dad, and I were on our way to get some lunch before going home, that Burnett wrote a message to an encrypted email address:

Odin displays signs of high intelligence but also extreme standoffishness, likely due to being in a new environment with strangers. His immediate interest in and lack of fear at looking out the window shows a curiosity about the world and an instinct to trust the word of others. No sign of unusual activity yet. I've instructed his handlers to cautiously begin message reinforcement as he acclimates himself to his new surroundings. Progress will continue as planned.

It was another two weeks, our third session together, before I spoke. We were playing the game again, me playing green and her playing yellow. She started the game by moving the leftmost piece one space toward the middle.

"You always start that way," I said.

"Do I?" That was her reaction after two straight weeks of silence.

"Every game."

"I should be easy to figure out then."

Looking back on it now she was specifically setting a pattern for me to notice. Repetition, it's the key to proper conditioning.

"I can win anyway," I said. "I remember every move you've ever made."

"Really?"

I nodded. "Last time you started the first game there and then you moved there and there," I pointed at the spaces on the board where she jumped her pieces to set a chain. "The second game you started there and moved to there and there,"

I pointed out the other spaces, the first two moves were the same, but the third differed. Variations from the origin.

"I'll have to try something different next time."

"Uh huh," I said, reaching to make my first move.

"Do you always start the same way?"

"No," I said proudly. "I started this way only one time before."

"When was that?"

"Second game two weeks ago." I then showed her every first move I made in every game we'd played since our first session. Then every second move.

"You have a very good memory, Odin." I nodded, again quite proud. "How do you remember these things?"

"I imagine them."

"Do you remember anything else?"

"Umm . . . like what?"

"Like, what did you do this morning?"

"Umm . . . I woke up, I watched TV, ate breakfast, and then I came here."

"What did you eat for breakfast?"

"Mom made me cereal with bananas in it."

"Was it good?" I nodded. She reached out to make a different second move than before.

"And your breakfast was yogurt and fruit."

She stopped, still stretched to finish the move. "How do you know that?"

"I imagined it."

"That's . . . quite an imagination."

"My friend said it makes me different from everyone else." I made my own second move, one that I had done before, but not in sequence with the previous move.

"A friend at school?"

"No, a friend who I saw one time but not anymore. I only hear him now."

"Is your friend in the room?"

"Yes."

"What's your friend's name?"

"Wendell."

"What else does Wendell say?"

"Just that I should remember that I'm different from everyone else."

"You are, Odin, but that doesn't mean you're better or worse, just different."

"I know."

"Good." She made her third move.

She wrote another message after that session:

Continuing process as planned.

It was the same message she would send after every session until two years later, when I stopped going to see her.

———⌣———

I take my time scanning through as much of her life as I can, skipping the parts that are irrelevant to me—time caught in traffic, the end of her long-distance marriage, grocery shopping, her post-divorce dating life, cleaning—keying in on moments when she was in meetings with Dad, or Braxton and Choi a few years later. Her statements were always short: "Mention it to him for three days and then ask again next week," "No cameras. Give him space," "Express pride and maintain pattern." She never gave any explanation or rationale for her instructions. She kept everything in her head, a place I can't reach. I can only live in my head, mine and no one else's. She and Delgado were only in the same room once before coming face-to-face in the lab that day. They had been in meetings together, but one was always on the phone, and others were present. There's no way that distance wasn't planned.

I lie on my bed, staring at the ceiling. Despite the faux wooden walls, the ceiling remains empty and white with the vent and lights molded into it. I wonder if I could crack that plastic covering over the bulbs, rip that vent off. But what would be the point of that? To let the gas in faster? Maybe I could cover it with the mirror instead. Form an airtight seal by removing the polished metal from the wall without bending it. Doubt I could do this, at least right now. I'd still be stuck in the middle of a small room, surrounded by armed troops, underground, in a prison, in the middle of an army base. The whole idea is stupid.

I sigh and look over my desk. The layout is different and there aren't any of the old toys, books, comics, and other clutter, but it's not that far from my old room. Bed, desk, no closet but a bathroom instead, which is preferable since I have nothing to store. Never had my own bathroom before, especially one that's cleaned every day. Toilets used to be called water closets . . . so there's also that.

I still can't go anywhere without being watched. I have no choice in my schedule for the day. Am limited to a monochromatic wardrobe. I eat when they tell me to eat. I go where they tell me to go. All-in-all, not much has changed from my previous life to this one. Alone, but after everything that happened, I'd probably be even more alone if I were still at school. It's far better to be alone when you're by yourself than when surrounded by people you once knew. Like Burnett said, this may actually be the best place for me. I sigh again.

She knows you too well.

"Burnett? Of course she does. She made me who I am."

Exactly.

"So . . . was that it? Was that your whole point?"

They do not know me.

"Feels like I barely know you and we've been living together for my whole life."

You know that I have never led you to harm.

"Never led me to harm? It's your fault I'm here." I kick my feet up and roll to sit on the side of the bed. "You fed me all this shit about my parents and some image of what I'm 'meant' to become, which started this whole thing."

It was all true.

I tried to think of an argument against that. None came.

I did not tell you to attack them or run from them. That was your choice.

"You pushed me to it. To fight Kevin, to attack Eric and them, Choi, everything."

I shook from his laugh.

It is always someone else with you. You are always the one being manipulated.

"Well, yeah," I say, "that's kinda been the problem."

Very well. You say it is my fault you are here. Then I will get you out.

"Bullshit."

I know more about your reality than you ever will. I have had years to do nothing but observe and practice. I have shaped and reshaped my own world hundreds of times.

"So then tell me, oh, mighty sensei, what do I do to get out of this place? And what would be the point of getting out of here anyway?"

The point is that you are not meant to be

here. You are not meant to be a tool of those less valuable than you.

"Sounds like you've been reading too much Nietzsche."

There's the jolt of laughter.

That was funny. You think I do not appreciate that but I do. It also does not help the situation.

"Now you sound like Delgado."

You have learned to let go of restrictions in your mind. This makes you powerful. Now you need to learn to let go of your body. Let yourself pull away. Just a little.

"Are you going to tell me to breathe deeply, find my center, and go into tree pose?"

If you like.

"Why would I want to do this?"

A demonstration. Something to remember when situations seem hopeless.

"Fine." I actually do close my eyes and focus on the shapeless black underneath my eyelids, as I did in the bowling alley. I imagine the world itself there in the black, a large spot growing smaller as I pull away. I feel my chest rise and fall with every breath, the floor beneath my feet, the equal force of my body and the bed pushing down and up against each other.

Look.

I open my eyes. Nothing has changed. There isn't a stack of pizzas in the middle of the room. I don't wake up in my old bed with vague memories of having the weirdest dream. There isn't a big party with everyone yelling, "Surprise!" and telling me this was all an elaborate birthday prank. I'm in the same room with the molded ceiling, bolted desk with sliding chair, bed, pillow and sheets, same orange uniform.

My finger twitches. Right hand, ring finger, second knuckle. I don't feel it. It twitches again.

"Is that—"

Stay still.

The other fingers begin to move, minute muscle flexes at first, like nervous shaking or slight contractions following electric shock. Then the fingers start to curl, each of them, into a fist.

"What's happening?"

I told you. A demonstration. Do not move.

"You said you couldn't . . . "

I said I observe. Now is your chance to do the same.

My hand, if it can be called that right now, clutches. Usually I can feel the squeeze in my fingers and knuckles. Instead, I feel nothing, not even the phantom sensation that amputees and paraplegics report feeling in the limbs they no longer have or control. One finger pops up from the rest, the middle finger.

"Funny," I say.

Do not think of moving.

"That's what you wanted to show me?"

No. This is.

The fingers stretch out. They move in ways independent from one another. The pillow comes floating into my view. One finger spins and the pillow does the same, rotating in midair. Two fingers alternate and the pillow flips end over end. The hand closes and the pillow crunches in the middle, as though smashed tightly on both sides.

Now. Make a fist.

My brain send signals to contract the muscles in my fingers. The pillow falls to the floor with a low bounce. I feel the pressure in my hand again, the faint pulse in my thumb. "You told me you were displaced and couldn't return."

I said was an observer. That I am here to guide you. I can offer help when you need it.

"Is that why you chose a hand? To make a 'helping hand' pun?"

No. Extremities are always the most efficient and easiest to control.

"You've done this before?"

Yes.

"While I'm sleeping?"

No. Your brain remains too active during that time. Being unconscious of the world naturally causes your mind to feel vulnerable. Because of that it actually holds tighter to reality. You have to make an effort to loosen it.

"Then when?"

During times when you are less aware of the world. That is when I can feel your hold slip. It is how I knew.

"Like before sleeping? Or in the bowling alley?"

Different intent but similar process.

I rub my hands over my head. Every follicle of stubble pokes into my skin on both ends. "Fuck."

But I cannot do it on my own, Odin. You have to allow me.

"Good. I'll never do that again."

I am not asking you to. Just remember it. If the time ever comes. You are surrounded by ene-mies here, Odin. Never forget that.

I shake my head. He sees my vision going back and forth.

Anything that happens to you happens to me

as well. I have never done anything to harm you. I never will. I am the only one who can say that.

I lean my elbows onto my legs, the push on every limb is immediate. I've never been so acutely aware of my own pressure points. Seeing my body move without with my control was like a scene from a horror movie. My fingers twitching and bending, pointing and folding, and none of it by choice. With him in control, it was as though nothing was there at all, no skin, no muscles, no nerves, just an ending. A disconnection. That is the ultimate manipulation.

I am sorry. I merely thought you should know.

"Know what? That I have a ghost inside me that could take possession at any moment?" I stand up, for emphasis I suppose, even if there's no one else to see it. "That every time one of these stupid fucking tests pushes me too far, I could end up knocked completely out of my body?"

Know that you have an option. If you make the choice to use it.

"Oh gee, thanks for that. Really helpful."

I understand this is frightening.

"You have no idea. First you tell me that you're only an observer." I fling my hands up and down, noting air on my skin and the tension of my shoulders, biceps, and forearms, "Then, you tell me you can actually control me better than any of these fuckers could ever dream. How is that supposed to help?"

I can do things that you cannot.

I put my hands out; feeling the stress in my wrists, fingers, chest. "You're not helping your argument."

Think of it like a nuclear weapon. You hope you will never use it. But if the time comes where it is either your destruction or theirs, it is a good option to have.

"I'm not a weapon."

No, Odin. You are not a weapon. You are a ruler.

9

MORE CONCRETE SLABS. AFTER ALL THE CONTRAPTIONS they rigged up—basketball hoop, pressure gauge stand, an obstacle course of metal tubes— what impresses them most is the same trick that karate teachers use to show off how advanced their students have become. Break this board and people will applaud.

Behind the glass, Winger shrugs while saying something to Delgado. His words are not important. Delgado has his hands behind him. The tips of his mouth are turned down and his chin is up. He doesn't look pleased, but then, he never does.

"Odin," Winger's voice comes over the speaker into the testing lab, "what are you doing?"

I hold up one finger to silence him.

They wanted a show. They wanted to see more of the random destruction from the day before. Their data must have been amazing. They must have witnessed completely new levels of energy flowing into and out of the PCC at the center of my brain. They wanted more of that. They added a pair of blast shields for Perry and Hawthorne to stand behind for when the rubble started flying. Instead, I've decided to slow their process and show them they are not in control by giving them something entirely different.

I pause to study the picture again in my mind, an image from my European History text in sophomore year. The slabs are quite thin and difficult to get to stand on-end but once balanced it's not too taxing to keep them there, especially those with a capstone. It's a very different process to move and hold an object than to merely break it. Crushing, smashing, fracturing, it's one action and physics takes care of the rest. Construction, suspension, balance, require that every little piece find its place. Each item becomes a part of the larger image. It can take centuries to build, only seconds to destroy.

I scattered the fallen pieces first, the ones that have toppled over in the middle of the original image. I ignored the little pieces that broke off in favor of using whole slabs. It's not terribly accurate. I swing another slab over to cap horizontally on two vertical blocks. It should technically be smaller, but that would require breaking the piece, and I don't want to do that. Not yet at least. One more capstone on the outer rim and that should about do it. It's a bit vague, but they'll get the point.

I step back, feeling the electrode wires swing as I move, and put my hands up to present the magnificence. "Gentlemen," I say to all my observers, "Stonehenge."

There's a moment of silence. I like to think it's

in awe. Then Winger says, "Could you please stop wasting our time in here?"

"Of course this is just an approximation, but I'm sure you can appreciate—"

"Odin," Winger says, impatience in his voice, "We aren't here for ancient architecture."

"I know what you're here for."

Delgado's folds his arms. His expression is sharp enough to cut through the blocks I've so carefully arranged.

"Good. Then can we get on with it."

"You're here for the Parthenon!" I say.

Delgado turns to face Winger at his side.

"Unfortunately, we don't have enough blocks to represent all of the columns but we'll do the best we can."

I sit down to make it seem like I'm concentrating, instead I listen to the conversation they had up to a second ago.

Winger threw his hands up in frustration, then onto his head. He peeked toward Delgado nervously, then to the console, then Delgado. "He's still giving us data," he said. "This is still usable."

"It's nothing," Delgado replied.

"I don't know what happened."

Delgado grunted. "The doctor got to him."

Winger gestured back to the monitor displaying my brain patterns. "This is unlike anything we've ever asked him to do."

"I don't care about your studies." Delgado swung one hand in dismissal of Winger's entire project. "I care about having a reliable asset."

"He's still a person. He's going to think and act for himself."

"No," Delgado said, "he's a tool." I almost react to that. "And a bad one if he's unwilling to serve his purpose. We don't have time to waste on useless experiments. Not anymore."

I see myself through the glass blankly staring at the model constructed so carefully on the floor. Electrodes stick to the stubble on my head. It's still unsettling to see myself from outside, as other people do, or as I do when seeing them. Even stranger to see myself without hair. Not sure I'll ever get used to that.

"We have previous sessions," Winger contested. "Those should be enough to continue."

"We haven't seen how he reacts under pressure." Delgado stared at the side of my shaved head as though if he concentrated hard enough I'd burst into flames.

I hear the door slam from behind the glass a second before I see Delgado exit the observation room. Winger buried his face in his hands. I doubt he'll proceed without Delgado there.

"The doctor got to him?" What does that mean?

I begin dismantling my little monument. I pile the slabs back the way they were when I arrived. Word of my defiance will eventually reach Burnett. I wonder how she'll react. Maybe a walk outside followed immediately by Delgado slapping the shackles on me. Or a visit from my family before a warning that I'll never see anyone ever again if I don't prove more useful. Carrots and—

The observation side door slides open. Delgado steps inside. "Sir," says Perry, "firearms are not allowed—" He puts one hand out to hold her back.

Winger's voice fills the room, "General, you can't be in there."

Delgado strides confidently around Perry's post. He approaches the pile of concrete blocks. "Still think you're clever, boy?" he says, hands clasped behind his back as he walks. "Still think your friend the doctor will support you?" His eyes pierce mine.

"Why don't you ask her yourself?" I say.

"I never liked this project," he says, "not one bit. Then I saw the results and thought, maybe there is something here." He surveys the gridded walls around us. "The only lingering problem was you."

"General," says Winger again, "please don't contaminate our data set."

This is your chance.

Hawthorne emerges from behind the second shield, across the room from the first. "Sir?"

Delgado puts up one hand to silence him. He reaches to where his gun hangs just back from his right hip. "It's one thing to be so very clever in a controlled environment like this. Predictable. No pressure."

I flex my jaw at him. He's watched me every day for weeks. He knows what I can do. He should know better than to walk into a room where there are twenty objects I could use to cave-in his skull.

"A lot of people are so very clever when they feel there's nothing at stake. Then they fail when there's the slightest bit of adversity. But you aren't one of those people are you, Odin?"

Do not hold back.

I say nothing. I feel my teeth pushing against each other. My nostrils flare. My eyes narrow. My heart thumps like a bass drum.

"No, you're worse than them. You're someone who is capable of doing whatever is necessary, but refuses too."

Show them.

"This makes you useless."

They do not control you.

"And I have no tolerance for useless things." Delgado's right arm whips from behind him.

Weapon.

The flash comes before the shot. There's a blur. I close my eyes. I flinch. I feel the hot wind. I hear a *whizz* as the bullet passes my ear. An inch away. There are screams from all directions. I look back to see the small hole in lower right corner of a grid square on the wall behind me.

Delgado rocks with a single breath. "Never was good at that stance." He raises both arms. I see his one eye through the iron sights of the pistol. Smoke explodes from the barrel. The sound is a tiny shockwave. The bullet's tip reflects golden light. My fingers twitch. The bullet hits the ceiling. A hole halfway between us. Then, at last, I exhale long and deep.

Delgado's eyes narrow into blades at the edges.

His lips curl into razors. His irises, black diamonds, glance away from me. He nods at Winger.

"Got that?"

He holsters the pistol as he turns back to me. He seems to smile, but it may just be the shadows over the points of his face. He walks to the subject side door. I hear Rogers and McPherson straighten as the exit opens. "General?" Rogers says as Delgado passes. The door closes behind him.

Silence. Mouths open, eyes wide, frozen in terror and bafflement. Winger and the others look like the kids in the class who watched the teacher punch a student.

My fingernails dig into my palms. The vein in my neck throbs. The muscles in my jaw ache. My teeth press hard against each other, equal in their force. I push out one breath and release the tension from my head to my fingers to my legs. I could have died. That fucker shot at me! Like, with an actual gun. Twice!

"That was . . . that was not . . ." Winger struggles over the speaker.

Perry steps cautiously from behind her blast shield. Hawthorne leans out.

"I had no . . . ," says Winger. "He never said anything—"

Adrenaline. Fear. Anger. Every part of me shakes.

"He was only supposed to observe. That was the agree—"

"He fucking shot at me!" My voice squeaks as I scream at Winger behind that protective glass.

Perry rushes to the observation door. Hawthorne runs to catch up with her. Winger places both of his hands onto his head. He digs his fingers in, gripping fistfuls of hair.

I could have died. Actually died. One hit and it was over. My life, everything I've done, everything I hope to do, everything anyone hopes for me to do, even their experiment, over and done, and that's it forever.

I feel myself folding, falling, knees first to the

floor. My leg hits the ground, like they did during the fight on my last day outside. The day when Eric said he would kill me. He had no idea. No one believed that. But this. Guns are made to kill. There is no other reason to fire one. Delgado had spoken to me about assets and uselessness. He said these tests would save lives. Then he shot at me. I sway back and forth with every quick breath. There's an impact pain in my leg. Minor. Nothing in comparison.

"Odin," says Winger. The electrode wires hang along my back. They anchor me to the floor. I don't even care to pull them off.

"Get me out of here."

Winger says something over the speaker again. I don't hear him.

"Get me out of here."

We will.

The door on my side begins to open. McPherson peeks through to see me slumped on the floor in the center of the room. He motions for Rogers to lower his weapon.

We will.

We pass pairs of soldiers on the way into and out of the elevator. Another pair at the turn toward the medical center. Two more at the intersection between the mess and my living quarters. There are others on patrol. They're not even trying to hide that the place has become like the streets of an occupied city. McPherson and Rogers seemed almost sympathetic in the lab, but among their brothers-in-arms, they are stoic and silent. They march with no concern.

I hear stomps down the hallway behind me as we turn toward the lock in front of the common area. Echoing stomps, sliding screeches, and "Let me go! He has to see me!"

A mass of soldiers gathers in a blur. Between

them I see Dr. Burnett, eyebrows raised and nose scrunched, shouting, "Let me through!" I turn to her. One step. "Odin!" The guards hold me back. "Odin!" My escorts pull at me. In the gap between soldiers my eyes catch with Burnett's. They speak of desperation. She rubs madly at the back of her ear as five soldiers finally shove her around the corner and into the hall toward the med center. McPherson and Rogers keep their hands wrapped about my arms, almost completely around my thin biceps. McPherson scans his hand to open the last locked door between here and *my* room. They push me in, unevenly, and block the door as it slides shut.

"I guess there's no chance I could go back out there." I say.

They don't reply.

"Looks like another lunch conversation is out of the picture."

They don't move.

"Have it your way."

They don't do anything.

I walk to my apartment, expecting them to follow. They don't. Instead, they remain right in front of the door where the common area and the apartment split, backs to the metal, eyes on me. I go straight to my room and slam the door.

It was this morning when Burnett most recently made the same ear-rubbing motion. She was in a room slightly smaller than this one. There were the usual plain, white walls, but with two bunk beds on either side of the room. She waited until two others were gone before reaching across her body to rub her right ear with her left hand. She sat on the bottom bunk and stared at the floor three feet ahead as she spoke. On the bed behind her was an open suitcase topped with a plastic bag of toothpaste, soap and other essentials.

"I don't blame you for not trusting me," she

said. "I probably should have expected that after everything we'd done to you." At least she acknowledged her wrongdoing. That's a start.

"You may not believe this but absolutely everything I've done, from the moment you came to my attention, has been for good." She kept her hands folded in front of her and her head down. "Or what I thought was good." She closed her eyes as though in prayer.

"I'm an idealist—in fact my professors, years ago, would say that I was too much of an idealist—but it's what I've always been. I believe that science, all sciences, should be used to benefit people. That's why I became a neurologist. I thought that the more we know of the brain, the more we could help people. Child psychology allowed me to put that theory into practice. I got involved with Solar Flare for the chance to work with exceptional children, like you. To help them grow and become the amazing people they were meant to be. When we finally found one, it was like my purpose was clear.

"I probably should have known better, but in my heart I truly believed that everyone else involved in this project felt the same way, especially now, when we're so close to achieving the goal we'd set out to accomplish all those years ago. I'd hoped that the research we'd conducted together, as . . . difficult as it may have been for you at times . . . would persuade them to allow the project to continue as planned. You may not believe me, but Solar Flare, the machine we were building, really was intended to be a boon to all people. There was never any malice behind it until . . . " She opened her eyes. " . . . It was a gift . . . " She wiped her face and composed herself before starting again.

"Solar Flare, both you and the machine, has been repurposed. I suspected it, especially after Delgado finally showed interest in our studies after your arrival, but I received confirmation from one of his underlings this morning. The bastard never even had the balls to speak to me in person. He wants to see the absolute extent of what you can do in order to allow Solar Flare to serve as a weapon, something that can level entire cities in one strike. Something as powerful as the bombs which struck Hiroshima and Nagasaki, but undetectable, unstoppable, and without the radioactive fallout. I guess waiting seventy years for a follow-up invasion is too much."

She shook her head. "Every breakthrough in history has been used to further the science of war." She stared at the lines in her open palms and bent fingers, as though watching something run from them: sand, water, blood.

"This is not what I wanted. Not at all. I told them this from the moment I joined and they assured me. Director Daschel, Braxton's predecessor, gave me his word. You would have liked him, Odin. He was a good man." She raised her head and exhaled slowly.

"I knew . . . I knew this was a possibility as soon as Braxton came in and Delgado was appointed liaison . . . but I had hoped that showing the good we could accomplish would be enough. I knew," she closed her eyes again, squeezed them until the crow's feet at the corners formed cracks stretching to the very ends of her face, "more than anything I'd ever known before, that seeing all the amazing things you and Solar Flare and the entire project were capable of—the technology, the knowledge, the redefining of our universe, the promise of a great understanding—I knew it would appeal to some innate, perhaps foolish, sense of good that exists in everyone. The same sense of good that I knew would come out in you if we did our job right." She released the tension in her face. Looked almost placid. "I mean, I know it wasn't perfect, but you turned out pretty damn good if I do say so myself. Even if you don't believe a word I say."

She brought her elbows to her knees and her forehead to her hands. "Always been too much of an idealist." She pushed her palms against her temples and lingered there. "Too much of a goddamn idealist." Shook her head with her hands. "They perverted science yet again."

She drew another quick breath and sat up.

"I wanted you to know this, even if you don't believe me. I don't know what to do or how to stop it. My main job was to handle you and now they say I'm no longer needed. They say they're sending me to Washington, but I don't know. I can't trust them either. I do know they haven't yet completed the conversion of the machine from an energy source to a dispersal mechanism, and the mapping hasn't reached the point that they hope it will. They want to continue with high impact situations, encourage you to push into more aggressive action, things that appeal to your feral instincts. Kill or be killed. That's what Delgado is hoping for after your previous display. They want you to enjoy this power. Maybe . . . I dunno . . . maybe if you fail or respond poorly it could delay their results. It could give me more time to persuade Braxton or demonstrate that the technology isn't fit for weaponization." She whispered, "If that's even possible." She nodded. "Or, if worse comes to worst, I'll try to wipe out the data myself. Even if it means . . . "

She looked up at the door, craned to see if anyone was on the other side of the window.

"I'm sorry, Odin. I know I say that all the time, but it never stops being true. Maybe none of us should ever have tried to interfere with your life. Maybe this is what we deserve." She stopped speaking again. She stood up, straightened her jacket and the front of her pants. She stretched her arms in front of her, spread her fingers and rotated her neck back and forth. She looked through the door window and saw that shadows had grown. "I'll see you soon." The door pushed open. Three soldiers approached her.

———⌣———

I feel the cold metal door on the back of my scalp. I look down at my hands, the healed cuts invisible among the deep lines and the tiny cracks that splinter through them. I touch the crescent outlining the orbital socket on the left side of my face. The level change in the skin, a carved dent, a memento to carry with me forever. My own scarlet letter.

She finally understands.

"You believe her?"

Yes.

"You saw what I saw?"

Yes. All of it and more.

"You told me—you convinced me not to trust her."

She has changed. They have not. You need to get ready.

"Ready for what?"

What needs to be done.

"I don't know that means."

You do. You do not want to admit it.

I close my eyes and breathe hard. Delgado appears in that darkness. I stare straight down the barrel of his gun.

If you cannot do what is needed . . .

The gunshot rattles my bones.

I can.

10

I<small>T'S LIKE SITTING IN THE CENTER OF MODERN ART,</small>
seeing the perfectly angled lines meeting each
other at equidistant points all the way across the
floor and up the walls and the ceiling. Mr. Woodley, the sophomore geometry teacher, probably
would have loved it if his room looked like this.
Gridded walls would have made explaining angles
and lines measurements so much easier, at least at
first, when everything is square and contained and
perfectly simple. Breaking out of those parameters
makes things a bit more difficult.

I remember having Richard in my geometry
class that year. We used to talk in the back while

Woodley was turned to the board drawing different shapes for measurement. Richard would yak about old *Simpsons* lines, girls in other classes, or his new dog. I'd ask questions for him to springboard off. Woodley would turn around and we'd immediately go quiet.

Then one day, Woodley walked up to me in the hall and asked for a word. He said that I really needed to stop talking during class. Not for him or even for me, but for Richard. He said, "You obviously have no problem with the material. You could probably skip all the homework and spend the whole class staring at your phone and still figure out the answer to every question. Richard can't. Talking to him is only making it harder for him to understand. Got it?" I nodded and for the rest of that year I didn't ask any questions. Richard would still talk about quotes, girls, and dogs, but I gave him nothing more. At times, I'd shush him up and say I was trying to hear the lesson.

He'd roll his eyes and comment something about, "What's the point?"

Eventually he got his grade up to a C+. Mine was an A. I didn't even need to try.

I can just about reach the grid lines at my sides with my hands. It's how I tell that I'm in the exact center of the exact center square of the room, the focal point of everything around me, contained in my proper place. On the floor with my legs folded, I feel like the standout in the middle with everything else building out from me. It feels extraordinarily appropriate right now. Too bad the electrode panel is placed slightly off-center. It throws off what would otherwise be a striking balance when I picture it from above, if not for the metal plate with a series of soldered posts as a sort of slalom/labyrinth placed on the floor and the assortment of different metal objects in front of me. Maybe that's why Mr. Woodley's class sprang so immediately mind.

"Odin," says Winger over the speaker, "the

sooner we finish the test the sooner we can all leave."

"Why?" I say, putting my arms out as I turn to face him. His head is barely visible behind the console from my place on the floor. "I'm actually enjoying this for once. You get a whole different perspective down here."

Winger rolls his eyes and mutters something to Perry and Hawthorne, who are in the room with him. Perry scratches at her fingernails while Hawthorne spins in his chair. The general isn't there. He and Winger talked this morning about whether or not he should be present. Delgado argued that without him, I'd be more likely to continue this ill-conceived protest, his words, and that I needed to be reminded of the consequences of such conduct. Winger countered that his presence would only add tension to the situation. Delgado eventually agreed to give Winger's idea a chance. For today.

"Send a message to the general," is what Winger said. "Are you even listening to me?"

"Yes, sir," said Hawthorne, immediately stopping his spin and assuming typing position at his keyboard.

"Tell him the subject is continuing to refuse to participate in the daily tests. That he is being uncooperative and intransigent."

"Intransigent, yes," Hawthorne said.

Winger faced them, "You know what, I'll write it myself. You guys go take a break."

"Are you sure?" said Perry, not even looking from the last bits of polish left on her fingers.

"Go ahead. We won't get any data today."

Perry nodded. "Would you like anything from the mess, Doctor?"

Winger shook them off. Perry and Hawthorne left. Winger reached for the laptop on the desk next to the main console. Funny, I've never run into any of them anywhere outside of the testing lab. Probably scheduled that way. Don't want them thinking of me as a person.

Winger typed his message:

Subject continues to be uncooperative and intransigent, refuses to take part in daily testing. Suspect he resents the nature of testing. Please recommend action.

He hit send, closed the messenger program, and slid over to resume staring at me sitting in the exact center of the room. No shattering blocks or tossing projectiles today. It was navigating different metal objects—one of the ever-present balls, a cube, a pyramid, and polyhedrons of six, eight and twelve sides, like those dice sold in comic book shops—through the maze of metal posts sticking from the plate in the floor. They wanted to see how my mind reacted to the varying shapes, the motion, and how many objects I could handle at once. Begin with one, then add another, then another, over and over through different paths, but always running the same course. Rats in a maze. I shuffle forward a little more to keep myself as close to exact center as possible before lying down on the floor.

"I'm going to start thinking about puppies now,"

I say out loud so Winger can hear me behind the glass. "Tell me which part of my brain lights up when I think about puppies."

Winger says nothing.

"I bet it'll be the part that handles sense of tactile awareness and adorability."

He sighs. "If you refuse to participate, you will be confined to detention until you decide to resume cooperation."

"That's fine. Fewer distractions while I think about puppies."

Winger shakes his head. "Fucking punk," he said without pressing the speaker button.

Better this than the alternative, Doctor, trust me.

———⌄———

There's already a pair of guards stationed in front of the elevator across from the testing lab. Another two stand at the door to the fabrication area, the point beyond which no guns are supposed to be allowed. The nature of the change makes me wonder why they decided to even try making it look gradual, as though I wouldn't notice that, day by day, there are more armed guards flooding the area. Or maybe they wanted me to notice. Make it feel like there's nothing I could do to stop it.

It's still just McPherson, Rogers, and me in the elevator up, but once the doors open, it's nothing but soldiers at every turn, down every passage, around every corner. I see more of them in the medical center and the mess hall. Perry and Hawthorne don't appear to have made it to the mess. There is no science here anymore.

The greatest concentration of soldiers is gathered, either standing or in motion, in the waiting area in front of the door to my quarters. No surprise. I wonder if all of them have their finger and palm prints encoded into the lock, or if that's still a right reserved only for my personal escorts, Delgado, and possibly others. Maybe they've decided it's better to keep me contained in one place than controlled in that place. No matter.

We walk in. I look down the passage to the room of my apartment. No sweat today, not tired, no reason to go in there right now. Besides, the common room is the better place to greet the visitors who should arrive soon.

McPherson and Rogers stop at their normal places right outside of the common room entrance. No one has spoken to them about any change in protocol. In fact, looking into it, no one has told them anything at all about their detail other than to not allow any civilian contact with me outside of the testing lab. Even in the mess hall. That was their last order three days ago, shortly after Burnett was restrained in the hall outside. Nothing since then.

I take a seat on the couch in front of the television. McPherson and Rogers keep their eyes on me, as they do any time that I'm in the same room as them. It's the same with Carter and Harris, the afternoon shift. "TV on," I say. The voice command has never worked terribly well. "TV on," I say again. The set takes a moment to warm up before the selection screen appears. I pretend to look through the different options.

I think there's a night watch of soldiers as well, but I've never seen them since the whole complex goes into lockdown at midnight. Even the door to my room, with its standard handle, has a pair of bolts inserted on both sides. "TV next page," I say, as though I'm looking at the titles. I don't imagine it'll be too long now. Real question is, where's the best place to begin? The bolted table with the sliding chairs near the locked game and book cabinet? The fitness area with its cardio machines also screwed into the floor? Or here, the couch in front of the television? Maybe find some appropriate background noise?

Too bad there isn't a spinning chair to use, like a Bond villain. That would be fun. Of course, that would also imply that I'm the villain. And I'm not. I don't think I am. I'm not the one building a weapon capable of leveling cities or holding a juvenile in an underground facility against his will. I'm not the one who attempted to control another individual and mold him into exactly the type of docile creature who will do what I want and nothing more. But I am the one who's made it possible for them to build this weapon, made them design an entire program to shape me. I am the reason all this is happening. I'm not the villain. I created one.

The table is probably best, side against the wall, like the last time Delgado and his entourage were here. Good to have space between me and them. I sit down just as the door begins to slide open. A second ago, McPherson and Rogers straightened against the wall. "Privacy please," Delgado said. Rogers immediately stepped out. McPherson paused a second, then did the same. I hear the rest of Delgado's group enter.

Prepare yourself for what you know you must do.

Delgado walks into the room as though nothing could possibly harm him. He gives me a look that's like stabbing someone in the chest just to see their reaction. His eight bodyguards fill in behind him. The eyes are the only human thing about them. Must make it easier to command if you don't think of those in your service as people.

I fold my hands in front of me on the table and look up, trying not to shake too visibly. It's not easy. I've poked the bear, now I have to hope his claws aren't too sharp.

Delgado looks around at the room, the other places where I could have chosen to sit, to the track chair on the other side of the table. "Symmetry," he says to me. "Have it your way." It's still strange how melodic his voice is. Almost like he's singing a pop chorus. He slides the chair back and sits. The soldiers fan into a half circle behind him.

Be careful. He fears you.

He starts. "As impressive as your little magic bullet trick was yesterday, I doubt you could do it again at this range with twenty rounds aimed directly between your eyes."

"Maybe with a bit more practice," I reply, with all the bravado I can manufacture.

He runs his fingernails back through his hair. "I'm sure by now that your friend, the good doctor, has filled you in on the changes to the project. It was an absurd ruse to begin with."

They all fear you.

"Where is she?" I ask. "Dr. Burnett?"

"You don't care enough to look? Or are you not as mighty as rumored?"

His statement confirms that he knew I could watch him. That could be why he never interacted with Burnett. Question is, how did he find out?

He believes his weapons and rank protect him.

I want to focus on her, find out where she is, but one glance at the guns lined up behind him reminds me not to give even the slightest indication that I'm using any of my abilities. Not yet.

His protection is an illusion. He is not strong enough for order. He can bring only chaos.

"Your friend, the doctor," he says, "has been relieved. She's been reprimanded and returned to her comfy little life."

He presses back, moving like he wants to tilt the chair, but the track holds it in place.

We will show them order.

"See, this is what I've missed about this assignment," he says. "Being face to face with the enemy. Looking at them directly. None of this hiding behind intermediaries and subordinates. I like to know exactly who I'm dealing with."

So I am the enemy now?

"So I'm the enemy now?"

"You haven't been an ally. You could be. In fact you were for quite a while, but it seems you've decided to change sides."

I look over the faces of the soldiers behind him,

the small, empty eyes peering from between pieces of military gear. I wonder how many of them have killed, how many lives they've taken. How do you ever come back from that?

We alone are strong enough to provide real protection. To save this world from itself.

"There is not a nation in the world that wouldn't use you the same way we have. At least here you were treated with some dignity. We tried to reward you." He gesture outwardly. "But sadly, you proved too unreliable."

"Feel like I've heard that one before."

He chuckles in a short burst, like machine gun fire. "We tried. We gave you every opportunity to assist in this project. Or, they tried, your friend the doctor and her superior, Director Braxton. They insisted that we make it seem like you were aiding us of your own free will, or whatever that psycho-babble was. My furious objection was not enough to persuade them otherwise."

We can stop them. We can give them a purpose and a place. True protection.

"I suppose I should thank you for validating my suspicions. My thought was that people are untrustworthy by nature. Someone like you should never have been allowed to roam freely."

He is right for the first time. Humanity is untrustworthy.

"I guess you're more of an 'or else' type of person," I say. I hope my slight shake comes off as anything other than fear.

They will always find new ways to destroy themselves.

The lines around his mouth tighten, pulling up like strings on a puppet. "I'm more of a 'do whatever is necessary to get the job done kind of person.' I have commanded one thousand, seven hundred, twenty-three soldiers to their deaths because that is what was necessary. And I would do it all again in a heartbeat."

Pawns of the unworthy.

I look through him, to the mass of uniforms, guns, and armor behind. Single strips over their eyes expose the soft parts underneath. "You know they can hear you, right?"

"Now instead of commanding soldiers, I have you," he says the word as though it leaves a foul taste in his mouth. "Some child who so-called experts thought was an amazing asset to humanity. A kid these tree huggers and peaceniks think can save the world by offering free, unlimited energy." His tone is farcical, then serious. "But what happens after that? Once everyone in the world has access to this fantastical force, then there's nothing to stop them from making weapons on their own. We will have given them the means to destroy us. Just as we did with nuclear energy. Why should we do that?"

He is right again. They will destroy each other. Completely.

"Why should we surrender the greatest advantage we have for the naive dream of idealistic fools who have no idea how humanity truly works? Your friend—"

"Stop calling her that."

"—The good doctor, she may study the mind, but she knows nothing about what happens beneath the mind, where our basest animal instincts bypass this illusion of civilization. That feral biological function that commands us to conquer and destroy."

Chaos . . .

"That is what someone like me does. We protect people from themselves, from the very nature they refuse to acknowledge, so they can continue to pretend that there is no true evil in this world."

Cannot be stopped by chaos . . .

"They can concern themselves with which coffee flavor has the fewest calories or what shoes best reflect their qualities as a person, instead of who is plotting to kill them and how, or where their killer could be coming from. That's my job, and the best way to do my job is through the promise of destruction."

It can only be stopped by order . . .

"It's by having the biggest, strongest, most destructive weapons available. Weapons that put the fear of God in the enemy on sight. Because if there's one base instinct stronger than the desire to destroy, it's to protect yourself from being destroyed.

Our order.

"And in this respect, you are the biggest threat there is."

He lets that statement hang there, a noose dangling right above our heads.

Odin. This is enough.

General Delgado presses back in his chair. "I like this." He looks over each shoulder to the soldiers standing on the outside. "I never get to talk like this. It's very cathartic to get out all the frustration I've had to bury for so long because it makes other people uncomfortable. It's never fun having to hold back."

"I know the feeling," I snarl.

"I'm sure you do." He chuckles. "Fact is, that we have enough of this project completed that you are hardly even necessary. We probably should have been rid of you days ago. It should be considered magnanimous that we haven't."

We must act now.

"And why haven't you?"

"Fine tuning. Contingencies. Making sure that we've completely taken advantage of our asset while we still have access to it, and, when I really think about it, more than a little bit of loyalty and pity. You never want to willingly deprive yourself of something that could prove useful in the future."

If you cannot do what is needed . . .

"It's when that potential usefulness is outweighed by potential harm that it becomes necessary to reassess its function."

I will.

"I take no honor in threatening a child," he speaks lightly until, "but you're not really a child."

"No," I say, "I'm not. Never was."

Weapon.

"Never had that opportunity. Never been able to choose anything for myself. From being born, to being able to do whatever the hell it is I can do, to being conditioned and brought here to this room so you can use me for the only thing I'm really good for."

It is time.

I feel the muscles tensing in my hands. I make an effort to relax them. Pull away from this moment. See myself seated at this table. See him and the soldiers around him, almost filling the room. See the four walls of empty space underground. The roads, grass, hangars, barracks of Fort Colton somewhere above us all. I ease my fingers flat against the tabletop, allow my shoulders to drop, until they aren't there anymore.

Show them.

I make as little effort to speak as possible. "I never had a choice." I close my eyes. This is what was meant to be. "If this is what must be done . . ."

Show them their place in this world.

Every weapon in the room is destroyed. Crushed and twisted. Every weapon except one.

" . . . I choose to start now."

I open my eyes. The panicked soldiers pull the triggers on disfigured metal scraps. They twitch, twist, bump into each other. They flail helplessly. They groan and grunt confusion. Their eyes, the one part that exposes them as human, are wide with fear. General Delgado spins in his chair. Its legs bang against the track. He yells, "Fire! Fire, fire, fire!"

I look at him. Straight in the eyes. Drills aiming at him.

His bodyguards are a panicked, bumbling mess. They have no power. They are useless.

I feel nothing.

They do not control me.

You wanted a weapon.

"You wanted a weapon."

I will show you a weapon.

"I'll show you a weapon."